Penelope's Perils

I0445648

By: Leigh

Penelope's Perils

Leigh's Creations
PO Box 22353
Carson City, Nevada 89721
LeighsCreations.com

"Thou shalt not muzzle the ox that treadeth out the corn. And the labourer is worthy of his reward." I Tim 5:18 (I Cor 9:9, Deut 24:15

"Therefore, behold, I am against the prophets, saith the Lord, that steal my words every one from his neighbor." Jer 23:30

"...Thou shalt not steal, ... Thou shalt love thy neighbor as thyself." Rom 13:9, (Matt 19:18, Mark 10:19, Luke 18:20, I Cor 6:8,10, Eph 4:28, ex 20:15, Lev 19:11, 13, 18, Matt 5:43, 7:12, 19:19, 22:39, Mark 12:31, Gal 5:14, James 2:8)

" Render therefore to all their dues: ... honor to whom honor." Rom 13:7 "That no man go beyond and defraud his brother in any matter: because that the lord is the avenger of all such, as we also have forwarded you and testified." I Thes 4:6 (Lev 19:13, Deut 32:35, Prov 22:22,23) Scriptures complied by the Bluedorns, Triviumpursuit.com

Penelope's Perils

Dedication:

I first of all dedicate this book to the giver of all good gifts, Jesus. He gave me this story of adventure to share first through our church's family journal, and now, by this book, with children of all ages around the world. Thank You Lord, for Your wonderful gift of words that I may be able to share with others good and moral adventure stories.

~*~

Next I would like to thank my collaborators:

For Jimmy Tracy and his brainstorming which gave me ideas for plot twists and continuing story lines when I got into sticky situations or dry spells with no idea which way to turn.

For Betty Sue Tracy and Betty Wiltse whom were instrumental in editing and proof reading, both for my journal entries and for their compilation into this volume for publication.

And also for my co-workers who, though unknown to them, helped to keep me inspired and on track with their constant encouragement.

My heartfelt thanks to each and every one of you!!!

Penelope's Perils

Penelope's Perils

Table of Contents

Penelope's Perils

Penelope's Perils

Preface:
How a Boy Becomes
a Knight

Many a lady at some point in her life, dreams of a knight in shining armour riding up on his white steed and whisking her away to a world of romance and adventure. Just how did one become a knight in the Middle Ages? The following information leads you through the stages to knighthood.

Becoming a Page:
A boy usually of nobility was chosen for knighthood, but not always. A boy started on his way to knighthood at about the age of seven or eight. At this time, he was sent to a Lord's castle to be trained for knighthood. This young trainee was known as a page. During his time as a page, he learned about horses, armour and weapons. Because hunting was so important, a page had to learn how to handle hawks and falcons, as well as to cut up a deer for venison. Since a page was also expected to serve the meals at the knight's table, they had to learn how to carve the meat properly before becoming a knight.
Pages practiced fighting with a sword against a wooden stake, or "pell" to develop muscles needed in becoming a strong knight. A page had to learn to skillfully use a bow and arrow for hunting and often practiced this skill by competing with others. Pages also had to clean the coats of mail by rolling it in a barrel filled with sand.

A knight not only had to know how to fight in battle, but he also had to learn how to be courteous. The lady of the castle taught a young page manners and social graces. He would learn how to sing, play instruments and dance from the lady. The lady would also teach him to read and write.

A priest would give the page religious training and he would often teach the page how to read and write.

Becoming a Squire

At the age of fourteen the page became a squire. Squires had to follow their master on the battlefield to protect him if he would fall. From the 13th century, squires fought on the battlefield beside their knight.

A squire was responsible for dressing the knight for battles and tournaments. He was the knight's assistant and the only one allowed to help the knight. The squire was responsible for taking care of the knight's armour and weapons. He had to become skilled in the use of the armour as well as the weapons. A squire had to get used to wearing the armour so it would be second nature to him when worn.

A squire had to become skilled in using the lance, spear, or sword. He had to practice so that the lance did not run back through his fingers when he struck the knight. He practiced against a wooden dummy called a quintain. A quintain was a heavy weighted sack or dummy in the form of a human. It was hung on a wooden pole along with a shield. The squire had to hit the shield in its center. When hit, the whole structure would spin around and around. The page had to move out of the way quickly without getting hit and knocked off his horse by the weighted bag!

Becoming a Knight

When considered ready, generally between the ages of eighteen and twenty, a squire was dubbed a knight. This was often performed by the knight who trained him. On the eve before becoming a knight, the squire confessed his sins to a priest was given a symbolic bath and then he fasted, cleansing his soul. Dressed all in white he prayed and kept watch over his armour and his weapons in the chapel all night. The next morning he would be dressed in symbolically colored clothes - red (for his blood), white (for purity), and brown (for the return to the earth when he died). Gilded spurs were attached to his ankles and he was "girded" with a sword. By a tap on each shoulder with a sword, he was dubbed a knight, thus reminding him of his vows he promised to uphold. If a knight broke his vows or was dishonorable, he was stripped of his knighthood in another ceremony to bury him, because in the Middle Ages, " a knight without honour is no longer alive."

~*~

There were two other ways for one to become a knight. If there was a battle and the King needed additional men, he would knight a number of squires to have enough men to fight. Also, one could become a knight for showing bravery and courage in battle.

Printed from: http://tayci.tripod.com/boy2knight.html

11

Chapter One
Lady Penelope

Long ago when kings ruled the land and ladies fair were locked in their towers while their knights went out to war, there was a nobleman named Rolfe. Rolfe was a knight of great stature and mild manner. His notoriety came from the fact that he had single – handedly put to flight a marauding band of villainous knights and won the hand and heart of the Lady Madeleine; as he had saved her from being one of their victims.

Rolfe and his lovely wife lived in the quiet hamlet of Leedsfield, about four day's ride from London on a good horse. Rolfe was the Lord of the hamlet and had many servants that lived throughout the community and cared for his crops, herds and flocks in exchange for the privilege of a small piece of ground to farm for themselves. These servants were happy with the way Rolfe and the Lady Madelaine ran their hamlet, as they could earn the deed to their property after working it for the space of 25 years. No other nobleman in the county gave his servants this privilege of land ownership. But Rolfe and Lady Madelaine felt it made for more honest and faithful servants.

About three years after Rolfe and Lady Madelaine were wed there was an invasion of barbarians in the north, near the border of Scotland, and the King had called for all the knights to gather and prepare for war to rid the country of them. Lady Madelaine was great with child as Rolfe was readying his armor in preparation to join the King's forces. She was expecting their first child to be born about two months hence.

"Rolfe," Lady Madelaine began, "I know you have to go to the defense of our country, but I am afraid of being alone. Is there someone we can hire to stay with me while you are away?"

"My Lady, I too dread for you to deliver our child alone. I will go into the hamlet and bring the midwife, Glenneth, to stay until my return," Rolfe promised.

"Thank you, Sir. I fear you are far too kind."

Glenneth was very glad to be of service to Rolfe and Lady Madelaine. She had looked forward to this day ever since the two of them were wed. Her only request in coming was to be available to others if any emergency should occur during a birth elsewhere in the hamlet. To this Rolfe gladly agreed. And having installed Glenneth safely in the manor house, he left to join the King's forces in the north.

A fortnight after Rolfe's departure, a frantic expectant father rapped loudly on the door of the manor house. Cook, just finishing her cleaning in the kitchen, answered the door.

"Is the mid-wife about?" Inquired an anxious father to be.

"She is up stairs with her Ladyship," Cook answered.

"Send her right down! My wife is having a baby now and she needs help, right away!

Cook went up to the Lady's room and called for Glenneth. Seeing the father in such hysterics and as Lady Madelaine was six weeks from the supposed arrival of her baby, Glenneth went into the hamlet with this father-to-be to assess the situation and help with the delivery. Upon her arrival Glenneth found that the "baby" was in fact triplets fighting to be brought into the world, and stayed to ease their arrival.

Later that night a violent storm arose throughout the countryside. Rain came down by the bucketfuls with long and loud thunder rolls and lightening shooting across the sky making it appear as daylight for brief periods of time before suddenly getting dark all over again. With the arrival of the storm, Glenneth could not leave the hamlet and return to the manor house and Lady Madelaine. She would have been washed away by the flash flood running through the lanes from the water that had over run the nearby riverbanks.

Penelope's Perils

The fury of the thunder frightened Lady Madelaine and brought on her labour much earlier than expected.

"God in heaven," she prayed, "have mercy on this wee lamb about to be born. The time is much too early for its arrival into the world. Maker of all, ever be around my babe and keep it safe all its days."

Lady Madelaine, full of pain and much fear felt she would not live to see the babe she had carried the past 7-½ months. With Glenneth in the hamlet there was only the cook in attendance to assist her; Madelaine gave birth to a beautiful baby girl, but the earliness of the child and the terrible fright from the storm quickly drained the life from Lady Madelaine. Just before the dawning of the new day she lost the struggle with life and death and quietly left this world. Just before her last breath, as the rain stopped and the sun began to shine, she named her daughter Penelope.

Glenneth arrived about two hours after dawn and found the cook holding the new infant, trying to calm her crying. It was all she could do to keep from crying herself when she found that Lady Madelaine had died while she was away. Glenneth took the little Penelope from the cook and walked back into the hamlet. She knew of another family with a new son whose mother she would ask to nurse Lady Madelaine's daughter. Glenneth knocked upon the door of the cottage. A farmer opened it up and welcomed Glenneth and the wee Penelope inside. Standing in its singles room Glenneth addressed the farmer and his wife:

"Lady Madelaine has just passed into the next life leaving this poor lass no mother to nurse her young life. Ma'am would you consider nursing the child until she can be weaned and returned to her father's house?"

Looking into the eyes of her husband, the lady of the house replied; "We would be honored to care for Sir Rolfe's child. It would be a blessing and a privilege."

~*~

Penelope's Perils

The King's army was at war with the barbarians for the space of three years, in which time Rolfe could not come home to see his wife and child. He knew that the babe had been born, but knew nothing of the tragedy he would find when he arrived there, as there was no way to get a letter to him and no one to even write such a letter, because servants of the hamlet were not taught to read and write unless they were keepers of the household records, and Rolfe had always kept his own records. So upon his arrival Rolfe found his wife had passed on, but took comfort in the fact that he could dote on his beautiful daughter.

Time passed and Penelope was growing into a very beautiful girl. That she looked the perfect image of her mother pleased Rolfe very much. She had sparkling green eyes; which danced with fire, long flowing blonde hair, and was as lithe in body as the feathery limbs of the ancient weeping willow, which grew on the bank of the creek in the midst of the hamlet of Leedsfield.

As Rolfe had only brothers to grow up with and there was no Lady in the household, Penelope was being brought up in all the ways of a knight of the realm. Oh, there was some womanly influence brought in by the servants of the house, but these were just the basics, like how to comb her hair, keep clean and the basic duties of keeping house and cooking. Penelope also learned how to handle a sword and lance, how to ride on the back of a horse like the very wind, and how to hunt for game, herbs and wild berries that were edible in the woods and glens of the hamlet.

In the midst of Penelope's 15th summer, the King called for the knights to join him in London. It was to be a time of training and revelry, as there had been no threat from their enemies in many years and dragon sightings had recently declined. But the King wanted to know that his knights would be ready in the event of an invasion of any kind. Rolfe was wont not to go, but knew that to disobey the King was to lose one's life for an act of treason.

"Father, why can't I join you in London for the training and tournament? I can joust as good as any squire or knight. And I can shoot clean and straight. I would make you proud in any of these events."

"Penelope," Her Father replied, "While I admire all of these skills in you, the other knights of the realm would not approve of your participation. You shall remain home and learn a new recipe for guinea fowl or something. Don't pout now. It isn't becoming on a young lady."

"But Father, I have never been to the city. I have never even been away from Leedsfield. I would truly love to see London and the ladies of the court. I should like to learn how to be more of a Lady. Wouldn't this be grand?"

"I am sorry, my dear. I shall have no time to watch over you. The King has given me a great many responsibilities for this training and the tournament to follow. And I fear we have no female relatives whom I may place you in care of. You will have to remain home. I would like for you to learn more the ways of a Lady, however this will not be the time. I am truly sorry."

No matter the amount of pleading or tears from Penelope, Rolfe would not relent. At dawn the next day Penelope stood at the gate of the estate and bid her father farewell. The servants thought it quite strange that the young Lady shed no tears as Rolfe departed. But they were not privy to the secret she was holding in her heart.

When Rolfe was no longer visible from the tower of the estate, the young Lady Penelope disappeared. She went into her room and changed from the dress she had worn in honor of her father's leaving and donned the boyish attire she normally wore while out in the forests searching for the wild things to bring back to the estate's table. None of the servants thought this to be strange, as they were used to seeing her so clothed.

While the servants were busy about their duties, the young Lady slipped out of the hamlet on the back of her favorite horse, taking with her the sword that her father had used in teaching her the art of swordsmanship. Penelope was not missed until the servants were setting the table for the midday meal. When she could not be found within the confines of the estate, they thought she must be about the wood on some great imaginary adventure. They did not become concerned until nightfall when there was still no sign of her, at which time the cook sent the stable boy into the wood close by to search for her. He conducted his search for close to two hours with no results. About this time, the whole hamlet was up in arms as to her disappearance. The men folk thereabouts got together and sent out a search party, thinking that the young miss was lost or hurt in the fields or woodlands round about. When night was at its blackest, they left off until the breaking of the new day. They kept up this valiant effort for the space of three days.

Penelope's Perils

Chapter Two
The Journey to London

Rolfe had gone to London at the bidding of the King. Shortly afterward, the young Lady Penelope secretly left the estate to follow after her father and join him in London. The absence of Lady Penelope left the servants of the estate and the villagers of the hamlet very heavy of heart for her whereabouts and safety. And so we pick up the adventure as the villagers are continuing their search.

Meanwhile, Penelope has left the woods through which she started her ride, in order to remain undetected in her departure, and picked up the Post Road on her journey to London in search of her father, Sir Rolfe. She has ridden until twilight and is now in search of a place to stay the night until the new day dawns. Thus far her trip has been very uneventful, with only the passing stranger to pass the time of day. But as it is growing dark and there seems to be no village or country Inn nearby, Penelope starts to wonder where it would be safe to rest until it is light enough to continue her journey.

Just as the stars are beginning to shine in the night sky, Penelope comes upon a field in which there are many haystacks close by the road. Penelope dismounts her horse and leads it off the road toward a haystack near the middle of the field. She places the reigns of the horse under a rock, near the haystack, to tether him for the night and climbs into the hay to keep warm as she sleeps. Thus the passing of the first day of her trip has ended uneventfully.

At the dawning of the new day, Penelope remounts her horse and continues down the Post Road towards London. After about an hour's ride our young Lady is starting to get very hungry. So she starts looking for a roadside Inn in which to take a bit of breakfast. After traveling another half an hour or so, Penelope comes across a cottage near the road and decides to stop and inquire about getting something to eat.

Penelope's Perils

Just as Penelope dismounts she hears a scream from the cottage: "Stop, thief! He's stealing my animals, somebody stop him.

Penelope runs to find out what is going on. As she gets closer to the cottage she sees a dark figure running away through the near by woods carrying a chicken in one arm and a small pig in the other. At the door of the cottage is an old woman sobbing in fits of tears. Penelope drops the reigns of her horse and chases the figure to avenge this old woman.

The Lady Penelope quickly shortens the distance between herself and the dark figure, as she is rather fleet of foot and he is rather on the portly side and is breathing heavily from his run.

"My good fellow," Penelope begins, "what meaneth the invasion and theft of this lady's livestock?"

"This woman is greatly behind in paying her taxes to the landlord. He gave me orders not to return this day without payment of some kind for these taxes owed."

Penelope, still dressed as a boy, gave the tax collector the five shillings owed and enough more to pay for another year thus rescuing the woman's livestock from the tax collector.

"Thank you fine sir, for rescuing an old widow woman." The lady of the cottage said, eyes full of tears at the return of her precious animals.

"My pleasure, Ma'am," Penelope replied, "Anything to help a lady in distress."

"I am so grateful for your service today. How can I repay you?"

"Well, my lady, I had left the road seeking to buy a meal to refresh myself from my travels this day."

"Young man, I would be honoured to prepare a fine meal for you to reward your valiant efforts for my dear little animals."

As Lady Penelope prepared to eat her meal, she removed the hood covering her head and the woman was shocked to find a young Lady in all that boyish attire. So Penelope shared with her the tale of how she came to be on the Post Road dressed as a boy. And in return the old woman told Penelope how she came to be with no funds to pay the taxes owing on her property.

"My dear girl, my husband was up in years and has lately taken up residence beyond the blue skies with our Lord and Maker. And his Royal Highness, our King has taken my sons into his service as squires for two of his knights who had no sons or other male relatives to train for the positions. They are even now in London at the King's training grounds preparing for the coming tournament. As first year trainees they will get no income to send home to keep their poor, old mother."

Her tale stirred Lady Penelope so, that when she excused herself from the table to re-don the hood that had been concealing her true self, she took several coins from the money belt hidden beneath her tunic. As she went to leave she made to shake the lady's hand to thank her for the meal she had enjoyed. So doing she slid the coins into the widow's small, open hand.

"Thank you, kind lady, God bless and keep you all your days." Penelope said as she mounted her steed once more.

After the widow woman lost sight of Penelope's back she looked down into her hand to see what Penelope had given her. Upon opening her hand she found 10 guineas, enough to support her for the rest of the year and to hire someone to plant and harvest her fields for the coming one.

~*~

During this second day of the young Lady Penelope's disappearance, the people of the hamlet and servants of her father's estate kept up their search for her among her local hiding places. They looked throughout the orchards surrounding the estate and the many caves in the nearby woods, all to no avail. And so with the setting of the sun on the second day the servants of the estate sat around the table in the manor house kitchen discussing what their next course of action should be.

As they are deciding whether or not to send a messenger to the King's palace in London for Rolfe, the young Lady Penelope takes refuge for the night in the barn of a small country Inn as there are no rooms left and it has become too dark to ride any further.

Penelope's Perils

Chapter Three
Penelope and Gregory Save the King

At this point in the story I thought I would better acquaint you with the triplets that were born the same night as Penelope, as they are going to be more closely involved in the perils that Penelope is to soon face. The oldest of the lads, by a mere 2 hours, is Godfrey; he is the tallest and most athletic of this trio. Next is James, who is but 30 minutes older than their youngest brother. James is the scholar of the bunch and has his heart set on being the next vicar of the village of Leedsfield. Last, but certainly not least is George. George is by far the craftiest of the lot. He can think of things most people wouldn't dream of in their entire life.

~*~

When we last saw Penelope she was just falling asleep in the barn of a roadside inn on the Post Road at the end of the second day of her trip to London in search of her father, Rolfe. While she is sleeping, Penelope's horse nickers and starts to paw the ground as a noise outside the barn has awakened him. The rustling of her horse in its closeness wakes Penelope as well.

"What is it boy, what do you hear?" Penelope asks as she quietly gets up from her makeshift bed to investigate the cause of the noise, which has roused her horse. Just outside the barn is a group of three men talking in rather loud whispers, thinking that they wouldn't wake the people asleep inside the inn. But they didn't know that the Young Lady Penelope was trying to sleep in the barn just behind them.

Penelope, now fully awake due to their talking, looks out the barn door as it is open just a crack. There she saw three rather rough and dirty looking men talking quietly just outside. They were dressed in dark clothes with full-length cloaks, and masks covering their faces. Holding her breath, Penelope stands with her ear to the opening to listen. The largest one, who is doing most of the talking, seemed to be giving the other two instructions.

"We have about two more days ride ahead of us before we reach the castle in London. When we get there I want the two of you to gather all of the men together. When you find them, have them meet us at dusk in the graveyard behind the monastery three days hence. We want to be sure nobody knows we are there. This is supposed to be a surprise attack on the King while he is watching the knights in their jousting tournament 4 days from now. That doesn't give us much time to set things in motion, so we must ride both day and night taking a rest in the early evening until the moon is shining bright…"

At this point in the conversation they crept deeper into the woods to finish their plans and get a few hours rest before the sun rose again. Having slept a couple of hours, Penelope quietly walked her horse about a quarter mile from the inn, then mounted him and set off in earnest again toward London, her dad and the King. She must get there ahead of this villainous group to warn the King of the coming attack.

~*~

At the dawn of the third day after the disappearance of the Young Lady Penelope the good folk of the hamlet of Leedsfield called a meeting of all the men folk there about. After a good deal of discussion it was decided they must send out a rider to find Rolfe in London and tell him of the girl's disappearance.

"Look, we have studied the lessons of knighthood right beside our young mistress," James, the scholarly one of the triplets that shared Penelope's date of birth began. "We are young and fleet a foot and can ride like the very wind. You should send the three of us to search for Lady Penelope. We would be able to search more fully than one man alone could. And as we are not encumbered by the duties of a home or land to run, we would be the best to go."

"Men of Leedsfield," The stable-master of Sir Rolfe's Stable stood to address the crowd, "James is right, these young men would be best employed in the search for the young Lady and the locating of her father. They are young and virile and could ably protect

26

Penelope should they find her before they reach London and the tournament grounds were Sir Rolfe and the other knights are in training. We should send them off right away."

At this exchange the men of the hamlet were agreed, so the stable-master went into the stable to get mounts for the triplets and sent them in search of Sir Rolfe, the young Lady and their King. Taking a large saddlebag of food each from the Estate's kitchen the lads took off at once riding at a full gallop. They rode long and hard all day and most of the night until they felt that neither they nor the horses could go any further. They found themselves near the cottage where the young Lady had rescued the widow from the tax collector and decided to stop to ask for lodging. The widow woman cautiously allowed the young men to sleep in her barn, and having thus slept in the Estate's barn on numerous occasions from the time they learned to walk, they eagerly accepted, in return they fed and cared for her animals that evening to pay for the privilege. But they refused the meal that she offered them, as they had no money with which to pay her for it and being thoughtful young men wouldn't put her to that expense on their behalf. Rising with the sun, they continued their trip to London in search of Rolfe at great haste.

~*~

Penelope rode hard that night, all the next day and on into the night, taking a rest for about and hour to eat at midday and again just as the moon was rising high into the night sky. This served not only to rest and refresh her, but was quite a necessary respite for her horse as well. About 2:00 in the morning Penelope was getting so tired that she reigned in her horse under a copse of poplar trees beside a pond just off the road a short way. She pulled her saddlebag and blanket off the horse and sought a bit of sleep under a nearby clump of bushes where she and her horse wouldn't be visible from the road. She slept until the sky was just beginning to lighten towards the dawning of the new day and then continued on her journey to London at her heightened pace.

Penelope's Perils

Upon arriving in London about noon that day, Penelope went in search of the King to warn Him of the grave danger that she had overheard the highwaymen discussing while she was in the barn behind the roadside inn just a short 36 hours ago. She knew that He would be in the vicinity of the tournament grounds preparing for the competition of His knights to take place on the day after tomorrow. So she followed the line of knights and squires headed south to the outskirts of London. As Penelope was still dressed in her boyish attire she fit right in with their lot and soon found herself in the midst of a group of tents and temporary corrals for the horses of all the visiting knights. To her utter amazement the tournament grounds could have been a tent city for the size of it. There were various bands of knights scattered here and there, with their entourages in tow, clustered about like various neighborhoods across the vast meadow where the tournament was to be held. Each of these clusters had a cooking pavilion at it's midst, as well as corral and black smith area on the down wind side of that particular camp site. She had never seen anything like it before and stood there in awe with her mouth hanging open. About the moment that she noticed the Royal Pavilion, a young, would-be squire tripped over the baggage he was carrying and fell head long in front of Penelope.

"What in the…" The young squire sputtered as he fell headlong and scattered the heap of baggage he was attempting to carry for about fifty feet.

"I fear young man, you have tripped over me." The boyishly clad Penelope replied.

"I tripped over you," he began anew, "how could I possibly…" then he faded off realizing that he had indeed just tripped over all of the bags and equipment his brother, Sir Steven of Tyrol, had piled upon his thin frame. He had thought to fume at Penelope for being so clumsy and causing him to fall.

Penelope, sitting on the ground too by this time, almost could not refrain from laughing as the young man who had tripped over her was in a tumbled heap, with his cap askew. Once she was back on her feet, Penelope set about the task of rounding up all of the baggage this squire to be had had in his possession, and restacked them in his arms for the remainder of his walk through the compound. Only she kept a few of them to keep him from tumbling headlong once again, and together they walked across the compound, once more headed in the direction of the Royal Pavilion.

When the pair was about 100 yards from the Pavilion the young squire took a turn towards a rather dark looking tent, so Penelope followed. When the lad made to go into the tent, Penelope stopped. She wasn't sure she wanted to go inside as there were several rather loud voices coming from inside some of which she recognized, so she just stood there holding the baggage she had been carrying for the would be assistant. The boy went in and deposited the bags he had been carrying. He looked about for Penelope; when he didn't see her there behind him, he went back outside and escorted her into the tent to relieve her of the load she had been carrying.

Inside the tent Penelope saw the large highwayman and the others that had been with him in the woods near the roadside inn where they had been discussing the plans for their attack against the King. These men were now dressed in the common attire of the knights of the realm instead of their dark clothing and long dark cloaks. They were in the midst of a large group of knights and there in their midst was her father, Rolfe, whom she had come to London to find. As she now had the important task of warning the King utmost on her mind, she did not cross the tent and greet him. Instead, Penelope quietly backed back out of the tent and started once more towards the Royal Pavilion. Her resolve to save the life of the King was made the more firm, as his would be attackers were among his knights; and these were thought to be his most loyal subjects.

When Penelope reached the Royal Pavilion, there was a rather large knight dressed in his suit of light mail standing guard over the entrance of the large tent. She approached and made to go in but this knight stopped her.

"Young lad, do you have an appointment for an audience with the King?" He asked her.

"No, Sir." She began, deepening her voice in reply, "I have a matter of great urgency to discuss with his Majesty. Might I please be permitted to speak with him for the briefest of moments?"

"The King is much to busy to handle your trivial squabbles. Run along now and mind your master at all times in the future." Returned the knight shooing him aside in the process.

Penelope was not to be daunted in this matter. But thinking it wise to bide her time, she thought to wait for a moment when the King would be out among the people. So Penelope went back to the stand of trees at the edge of the meadow where she had tied her horse upon entering the tournament grounds. There she pulled her saddlebag and blanket off the steed and found a spot on the ground nearby for a much needed rest while waiting for the right moment to speak with the King. Once she lay down, it was only a matter of moments before Penelope was asleep.

Penelope slept for several hours. When she awoke the sky was beginning to darken on towards nightfall. Wiping the sleep from her eyes, she went in search of some water to wet her now parched throat. Penelope wandered further into the trees hoping to find a brook to drink from in order to quench her thirst. After about a 15-minute walk, she came across a small pond and quickly approached its bank to get a drink of its cool, clear water. Upon reaching the water's edge, Penelope heard soft sighs and groaning nearby. As she bent to get her drink she turned her head slightly. There huddled in a large bush was the squire in training she had met when she entered the tournament grounds. He was battered and bruised about his head and torso and was trying to hide there away from the eyes of his master, the large highwayman/knight who was seeking to harm the King.

Penelope, having forgotten her thirst, sat beside the lad to comfort him and hear the tale of how he had gotten in such a state.

"What is your name, please, and how did you come to be like this?" Penelope asked.

"My name is Gregory. And my brother, Steven, is one of the visiting knights in the tournament the King is holding. He and a group of the knights he has brought with him were sitting about his tent this afternoon and I was fetching ale to quench their thirst. Well, I happened to trip over the feet of one of his friends and spill a tankard of ale all over him. Steven yelled all kinds of profanities and beat me there in front of his knights and threw me out of the tent. So I crawled here to clean up and rest a bit."

"My name is Paul. Is your brother the big knight that was dressed in the brown tunic in the tent earlier?" asked Penelope, still dressed like a boy. She knew that as a girl her message would not be as widely received, as it would be from a man, so Penelope continued her masquerade.

"Yes, that was him. He is mean and cruel to me, because I am not as strong as he."

"I saw your brother a couple nights ago outside of the barn of a roadside inn. He was talking to a couple other men. I saw those men in his tent today, also. He and these men are planning to kill the king during the tournament"

Penelope shared with Gregory all that she had over heard that night in the barn behind the roadside inn. Her tale did not surprise Gregory; instead he gave a look of enlightenment at her words. He had known that Steven was planning something, as he had been going out late of an evening and not returning to the camp until it was almost daylight again. Now Gregory understood all of his brother's secretiveness, and right away he vowed to help Paul (Penelope) in her efforts to save the King.

Together Paul (Penelope) and Gregory gathered all of the squires there at the tournament grounds and led them back to the edge of the pond. When all were gathered there were about 20 young men and boys.

Gregory and Paul shared the story of the planned attack on the King with those now present.

"Gregory", Paul started, "Is going to be our insider. He will gather information from his brother's group of knights and keep us informed as to what they are up to. He is close enough to be able to hear what they are planning with out raising suspicions."

"Yeah, and Paul will stay close by the Royal Pavilion to be as near the King as possible. That way if he gets an opportunity he will be able to warn the King of the threat against his life."

It was also decided the others would act as go betweens between Gregory and Paul, and lookouts for the villainous group of knights and highwaymen. And if necessary, they would become a human shield in order to protect the King's life. With all of their plans formed the young men headed back to their respective campsites and the duties they had of preparing their Knight's equipment before the start of the tournament on the morrow.

After readying Steven's gear for the jousting event the following morning, Gregory spent a restless night among the evil knights that were in league with his brother listening to all their carousing just in case he might hear any new bit of information that would help them save the life of the King from the attack of these evil men. Paul, on the other hand, grabbed his blanket and saddlebag from his horse and found a place behind the Royal Pavilion in the shadows to lay and listen for whatever may come close by in the night. They both fell asleep in the wee hours of the morning when the sky is at its darkest.

Gregory had only just gotten to sleep when there was a stirring within their tent. He lay there quietly so that the men who were rising all around him wouldn't know he was awake. And as Steven didn't want Gregory involved in his evil plans, he left him there to sleep on. When the last of the men had left the tent and gathered around the dying fire a few feet from its entrance, Gregory quietly crawled out of the tent after them. He stayed close to the ground and snuck up behind them to listen to their final plans. This was just the break he had been waiting for.

When Gregory had the gist of their plans, he crawled back into the tent and slept until Steven came in a couple hours later kicking at him to fix breakfast for his band of men.

With his morning chores out of the way, Gregory went looking for Paul and the other young men. Once they gathered Gregory relayed all that he had heard at the fireside in the early morning hours.

"Guys, I heard the men talking of being in the stands at the tournament and letting the games proceed. They are going to attack the King during the presentation of awards after the games have ended. When the King goes to award the Grand Prize the knight who receives the award will bow and kiss the Kings hand. This is when my brother and his men will attack. Steven will shoot an arrow into the Kings outstretched arm to distract the crowd. Then two of his men will rush the dais and smuggle the King into a waiting wagon, stuffing a rag into his mouth to keep him from yelling out. Then they are going to tie him up and cover him with a tarp to hide him. The driver will leave the tournament grounds and head east into the woods to escape. Steven's knights and highway men are to meet together in a cave just off the Post Road behind a Roadside Inn."

"I know that Inn," Paul (Penelope) stated, "its behind the barn where I first heard Steven speak of his plan to kill the King."

"That's right. Steven plans to send a ransom letter to the King's bodyguard for $100,000 lbs. But they have no plan to really return the King. Once their demands are met, they plan to hang his dead body from the castle wall in London."

After hearing Gregory relay the details of the attacker's plans the group started making counter plans in order to save the King from this evil fate. It was decided that as each of the squires were released from the tasks set by their masters, they would roam the crowds on the opposite side of the arena from the Royal dais and be on the lookout for any of the evil knights and highwaymen who might be there waiting for the appointed signal to put their plan into action. As Gregory and Paul (Penelope) were the only ones of the group who knew who any of these evil men were, they were going to get as close to the dais as they could, one on either side of the King, to watch for the villains and signal the others.

~*~

The tournament had gone very well and the awards ceremony was upon them. All the squires were in their places awaiting the signal from Gregory or Paul (Penelope). The winners of the various challenges were assembled in front of the dais. Rolfe, Penelope's father was among them as was Steven, Gregory's brother and the leader of the evil knights and highwaymen. The King had awarded each of the gathered knights with a medal for the challenge they had bested and was about to name the Champion of the whole tournament when a disturbance arose in the crowd on the far side of the arena. Paul (Penelope) and Gregory caught the action at the same moment and signaled the youths scattered through the crowd who immediately set upon the villains and prevented them from shooting the King and putting their plan of attack into play. At the same moment, Steven lunged at the King, but Paul and Gregory jumped into the fray and kept him from reaching his destination. At this point the rest of the murderous band started to flee, wherein the band of squires closed in from all sides and impeded their progress.

The King, with Rolfe at his side in protection, demanded what the fracas was about. Gregory and Paul (Penelope), with Steven between them, stood before the King and explained the plan of the evil knights and highwaymen. At the same time the group of young squires, who had rounded up the rest of the murderous lot, brought all who were guilty before the King, as well. The King had the Captain of the Guard and some of his men take the prisoners into London and lock them in the tower.

Penelope's Perils

When all of the dust had settled, the King thought to reward all the valiant lads for protecting his life. So they assembled in front of Him and removed their head coverings. A hush fell over the whole crowd as it was realized that Paul was actually Penelope. Even the other young men of the group had no idea she was a girl as she had fought equally as they had in setting down the evil plans of Steven and his band. But the most surprised was Rolfe as he was staring into the eyes of his lovely daughter.

The King gave each of the squires a medallion for their bravery in protecting His life. When He came to Penelope, The King said: "It is with much regret that I must tell you I cannot make you a knight as your valiant efforts do greatly deserve. However I give you my signet ring in token of my gratitude for all you have done." Rolfe then hugged his daughter and the two of them had dinner with the King and His court, as did all of the squires who had aided in thwarting the taking of the Kind's life.

As dinner drew to a close the triplets from the hamlet of Leedsfield drew up their reigns in front of the Royal Pavilion. They asked the guard at the door where they could find Rolfe and were escorted inside. There they saw their master and his daughter sitting in the presence of the King and his court. After taking a minute to catch their breath, they recounted their story of how they came to be at the tournament grounds. While they were yet speaking a page was setting large amounts of food before them in order to refresh their bodies from their long hard journey. Meanwhile the guard had some of his men see to the care of their horses.

When they finished their tale, Rolfe and the court set about to tell of how Penelope and the group of squires had saved the life of the King. After all was told, Rolfe decided that the triplets and Penelope could stay the next day to allow the triplets horses to recover from the trip. But on the day after he instructed that they should go home. In the meantime, Penelope was introduced to the ladies of the court who were in attendance at the tournament and given the Royal Treatment for a full day before she was to return home.

Penelope's Perils

Chapter Four
Our Merry Band Slay the Dragon

Dressed once again in her boyish garb, Penelope mounted her horse for the journey home. She is now in the company of the triplets, one of which flanked each of her sides while the third rode slightly behind. As the group is setting to depart Rolfe comes up to give them a last farewell and bid them safety on their journey. It is just before dawn and much of the tournament grounds are still asleep after a long night of revelry and merry making.   Rolfe reminds them to stick together and to be watchful for highwaymen. After hugging his daughter Rolfe hands each of the riders a knapsack full of food for the trip and Penelope a small sack of coins to pay for their lodging on the way. Then he walks away to see that the guards are all on their toes and that the preparations for breakfast are under way, he doesn't want them to see the tears that are trying to fall from his eyes.   Thus our band heads off toward London and then for Leedsfield.

~*~

As the sun raises high in the sky our little group dismounts from their horses and finds shade beneath a large tree beside the road for a bit of a rest and refreshment. The ride through London was a bit uneventful as the town was just stirring from their nights rest. While eating a meal of cold roast pheasant and bread they hear loud noises and screaming coming toward them from the forest off to the west. Fearing that some one might be in danger, they drop their meal and run toward the screaming. As they break through the brush into a small clearing they see a pair of small children being chased by a rather large dragon. Quickly assessing the situation the triplets and Penelope take action to rescue the children.

"James you go left while George goes right and Godfrey runs in front of the children to distract the dragon," Penelope yells. "I will rush to attack him from the rear. Keep him backing up toward that boulder; I am going to climb onto it and kill him."

As Godfrey has blocked the dragon's advance on the children, they are now quite a distance from the battle they stand amidst a copse of trees watching the foursome attack the dragon from all sides. Captivated by the adventure of it all they watched the dragon being beaten in this battle that could have meant their very lives. After what seem like hours, but was only a matter of about 30 minutes, Penelope and the boys have defeated the dragon. As Penelope, now sitting atop the dragon, struck the death blow, the children ran into the forest to get their father and tell him all about their near death experience with the dragon and how they were rescued by the four strangers.

Now that the battle is over and the dragon has been beheaded, Penelope and the triplets have decided to take a rest sitting against the boulder that aided their victory over the massive creature. As they are leaning there against the boulder catching their breath the children return accompanied by their Father, who is the King's Gamekeeper. As his children were very excited by the happenings in the clearing he decided he should go see what the excitement was all about. When the little group arrived in the clearing they find the dragon laying beheaded and quite dead just a few feet from the boulder where the band of heroes now sit regaining their strength.

"Thank you for saving the lives of my children," the father began. "What a marvelous thing you have done in killing this dragon. However did you do it?"

"Well sir", James began, "It was Penelope's idea. She had us distract the dragon and get between it and your children."

"Am I to understand that the hero is a girl?" the gamekeeper asks.

"Yes, sir," George replies, "She is well trained in all the ways of a true knight of the realm."

"Well, I'll be," said the gamekeeper in awe, "I want to invite all of you to our cottage to celebrate the rescue of my children from the jaws of this dragon and the bravery of the four of you for saving them."

When they arrived at the cottage the Father sent one of his older sons to London to share this news with the King. The Mother had been setting out food from the larder to feed and revitalize the young heroes since the children and their Father had left to go see the conclusion of the battle the children had told them about. She had put out sides of pork and lamb, roasted chickens and pheasants, and vegetables of all kinds from their garden, along with the fresh bread she had baked that morning.

After the feasting the family insisted that their band of heroes stay the night in the cottage sleeping in front of the warm peat fire. Early in the morning their older son returned to the cottage in the company of the King and his honor guard, of which Rolfe was a part for this occasion. When all had dismounted from their horses and the King was seated in the best chair in the cottage, he asks for the foursome to stand before him and remove their head coverings. He thought to honor them for their bravery in rescuing the children and defeating the dragon. As Penelope removed her head covering the Mother gasped at the sight of a young lady dressed in such a fashion, for the children had told that it was she who had struck the deathblow that killed the large beast.

But seeing Penelope did not surprise the King, in fact he rather expected it after the way she had saved his life. The King gave each of the triplets a medal of valor for their part in saving the lives of his gamekeeper's children. But as Penelope was last to stand before him, he thought to do something that had never been done before.

"Young Lady," the King began, "This is the second time in recent days that you have been of valiant service to myself and members of my staff. I would like to bestow on you a very great honour, one that no Lady has ever been given before. Today in the presence of this company of witnesses I ask you to kneel before me."

While Penelope moves to kneel before the King; and her father, Sir Rolfe hands the King his sword.

Penelope's Perils

"Penelope, in the name the God of heaven and by the throne of England, I pronounce you Lady Penelope, Knight of the realm and an honourary member of the Kings Honour Guard," The King proclaimed as he set the sword on each of her shoulders and her head in turn. "Arise and be so honoured."

Penelope rose and the King handed her a package wrapped in red velvet. Upon unwrapping this gift Penelope found a pair of golden spurs, the sign of a true knight of the realm, which had preformed deeds of greatest courage and valour. That day the King had broke with hundreds of years of Royal tradition when he knighted Penelope there in the presence of her father, his Honour Guard, the Gamekeeper and his family. After the ceremony the King and his Honour Guard departed for London. They thought to arrive at the castle before dark had fallen.

Again there was much feasting and merrymaking in the gamekeeper's house as the foursome now joined by Sir Rolfe, Penelope's father, stayed as the family's guests. Upon waking in the morning Penelope, Rolfe and the triplets would resume their journey home to the hamlet of Leedsfield and the Estate; to go back to their normal way of life, well maybe.

Penelope's Perils

Chapter Five
Penelope's Perils Continue

If you thought that Penelope's Perils were at an end; you, and I, were wrong. For Penelope has not yet reached home. Neither has she passed into the next life. And so our tale continues, and where it may lead only the Lord God knows for sure.

As you remember Penelope, her father Rolfe, and the triplets were headed home to the hamlet of Leedsfield. As the group dismounts for a break about midday Rolfe has decided to go on ahead after their meal to check on the King's outposts throughout the countryside on his way towards Leedsfield and home. While they share some left over pheasant and bread from the previous day's feast he shares his plans with Penelope and the boys. When the meal is finished Rolfe quickly remounts his stead and heads off on his journey towards the hamlet. The young people take a about an hours walk in the stand of trees they have chosen for their respite, then they, too, remount to continue their journey

By now our quartet has started again on their journey home to Leedsfield. They have been traveling about an hour since their roadside respite. They had fallen into a good rhythm in their ride and were making good time. The merry band was just coming into a small village where all appeared to be calm and peaceful.

All of a sudden there arose a woman's screams of fear in the distance on the East side of the village. There were very few men in this village as most were still on their way home from the training and tournament the King had held in London for all of his knights and men of valor. What men that were in this village were of advanced years and unable to quickly run to where this woman was hollering on the East end of the community. So our merry band of four quickly turned to the East to find this lady in distress and relieve her of her worry. About a quarter of a mile from the center of the village was a cottage setting about 200 yards off the road. Beside the cottage was a nearly empty cistern around which the screaming woman was running back and forth in great fear and panic. This cistern was about 12 feet deep and had about a foot and a half of water in the bottom of it.

As our group dismounted James went to the woman and started trying to calm her to find out what the problem was. He sat her down and took his jar of water from his mount giving her a drink in an effort to calm her.

"My dear woman, what is the trouble?' James asked.

"My daughter was playing with her pet bunny and they have fallen into the cistern and I can't reach them. They have been down in that hole better than two hours. I have been calling and calling, but I haven't heard her speak for ever so long. Can you help them?"

"My good woman, we will do all in our power to remove her from the cistern.

James left the woman sitting beside the cottage while he went to talk quietly to the others.

George upon hearing the plight of the child instantly had a plan.

"James, you are best suited to keep the good woman calm while we rescue the child and her pet from the cistern. Godfrey, you and Penelope should go out back of the cottage to find a ladder or other means to reach the bottom of this pit. Meanwhile I will inspect the cistern for depth and stability of its structure."

Behind the cottage was a small barn in which Godfrey and Penelope found a large coil of rope. Godfrey carried it back to the edge of the cistern.

"Here, George." Godfrey said as he laid the rope on the ground at the edge of the cistern.

"The walls appear to be solid, however it is a rather small place. I feel Penelope should be the one to desend. She is the smallest one

43

here. Godfrey, you and I will lower her into the cistern. At the bottom she can tie the rope around the child and herself."

"That is a good idea, George." Godfrey replied, "Penelope, you should take off your hood to give you better sight and your shoes in order to have better grip to climb back out of the pit."

"Alright Godfrey, but don't tie the knots too tight, I want to be able to untie them at the bottom. You know you do tie the hardest knots."

The boys tied the rope securely around her and began to let her down into the cistern slowly. It seems to take the boys hours to lower Penelope to the bottom of the cistern, but it is actually only a matter of about 10 minutes.

At the bottom Penelope first finds the pet bunny and wipes its face with a little water to see if it is OK. Upon her short examination she finds it is bruised and shaken, but seems to be fine. The child on the other hand has a large bump on her head and is unconscious. Penelope safely stows the bunny in her tunic and sets about to bring the little girl around. She dampens the edge of her tunic and wipes the child's face while gently patting her about her head and shoulders, all the while speaking to her, to bring her out of her unconscious state. It takes Penelope several minutes of this to finally get the little girl to fully come around. Then she gets her to her feet and ties the rope securely around them both. When the rope is in place Penelope gives it two short tugs, the agreed upon signal for drawing her and the child out of the cistern. George and Godfrey pulled them out together. James and the mother have now joined the others at the edge of the cistern to watch, as the rescue operation is under way and the boys pull them up out of the cistern. At the top the mother impatiently waits as they untie the pair and when they are loosed she quickly picks up her child and dances around the yard with her in joy for the way our little band has worked together to rescue her daughter and the pet bunny; which Penelope has just handed to her small owner.

When the mother gets the little girl settled into her cot, she beckons our group into the cottage to thank them and invites them to share a meager meal with her and her daughter in reward for their saving the child and her pet bunny from the cistern. As they try to refuse the mother insists and they join her and the little girl for a dinner of cold lamb and wild greens and fresh bread with lots of butter and jam to spread on it.

As they finish their meal the sun is starting to set. Seeing it has gotten to late for them to travel on that night, the mother invites the foursome to spend the night. The cottage being too small to house them all, she offers the boys a bed among the hay in the barn for the night and Penelope a pallet on the floor inside the cabin with her and her daughter.

Chapter Six
Penelope And Friends Ride On Into More Perils

When last we saw our foursome they had just bedded down for the night at cottage of the woman and her daughter, whom they had rescued from the cistern. It was a peaceful night and all were very well rested in the morning. After a breakfast of fried porridge and eggs, they again set off for the Hamlet of Leedsfield and home.

~*~

Meanwhile Prince Gregory, the young man who had helped Penelope thwart the assignation of the King, has just seen to the execution of his brother's sentence in London. And having no family to return to, had decided to follow Penelope to her country home. He started on this journey about a day and a half after our merry band had left the Tournament.

Little did anyone know, but Prince Gregory was now the crown prince of the small country of Tyrol, east of Switzerland and north of Italy. His brother, Steven, had been the heir apparent until his assignation attempt on the King. Now he was hanging from the wall of the Tower of London for this offense.

But Prince Gregory wanted to get better acquainted with Penelope before he made the long journey home to Tyrol. Prince Gregory had thought that Penelope was so brave and courageous that he wanted to know more about her, with the intent of courting her and winning her hand in marriage. So off he rode toward the Hamlet of Leedsfield. He rode day and night in his attempt to catch up with Penelope and the triplets. He only stopped when utterly exhausted and to rest his mount for a couple of hours.

~*~

About two hours after our group left the woman's cottage, Penelope's horse came up lame. So Penelope and her entourage had to stop and rest the horses and inspect the foot of Penelope's mount. At first glance there appeared to be nothing wrong so they rested horses about 30 minutes then tried to return to the road to continue their journey toward home. But it quickly became evident to all that there was more wrong with Penelope's horse than they could see. Being miles from any village and there were no farms or houses nearby, they decided to make camp in the meadow at the side of the road. James built a fire and George and Godfrey did a little hunting in the nearby woods for a bit of game for their evening meal, while Penelope saw to the horses, tying them to a bush so they could eat and rest. As she was tying the horses she heard another rider coming fast down the road, so she walked to the roadside to flag down this rider to get some help for her mount. Alas it was Prince Gregory, the young man whom she had met at the pond near the Tournament grounds outside London, who had helped her stop the robber-knights from killing the King. He had ridden night and day to catch up with Penelope and her entourage since leaving London, stopping only briefly to rest his mount each day.

Penelope quickly waived him to a halt and asked if he knew anything about horses, relaying the problem with her lame mount. Prince Gregory, having been trained in all areas of a squire including the art of the smithy, took a look at the hoof of Penelope's horse. Seeing that one edge of the shoe had lifted a bit he pulled out a knife and pried it from the horse's foot. He found a small pebble lodged under the horseshoe which he deftly removed and trimmed the hoof with his knife. Then he pulled a hammer and some horseshoe nails from his knapsack and reaffixed the shoe to the horse's hoof. Having rescued her and the triplets, from walking the rest of the way home, Penelope invited Prince Gregory to join them in their repast and to accompany them as they continued their journey on the morrow, which he gladly accepted.

By this time James had a perfect bed of coal on which to roast the game George and Godfrey had gone after. So Penelope and Prince Gregory joined him beside the fire to await their return.

They weren't waiting long, about 30 minutes after having seen to the horse's hoof the pair returned with a quintet of quail and a pair of large rabbits for their meal. The four young men made quick work of plucking the birds and skinning the rabbits and soon they were taking turns rotating the spit on which their repast was cooking. In the mean time Penelope took some fresh fruit and rolls out of her knapsack to add to the cooking feast. The mother of the child and bunny they had recently saved from the bottom of a cistern had given them these as a reward for their services.

After all were sufficiently stuffed, Penelope wrapped the remains in the cloths she had taken the rolls from and placed them into the knapsack to keep for breakfast the following morning.

Prince Gregory banked the fire for the night to keep the wild animals at bay. Then the four young men rolled out their blankets at the edge of the woods while Lady Penelope laid out her bedroll close by the fire.

Penelope's Perils

Chapter Seven
Penelope is Stolen

While Penelope and her entourage lay sleeping there was an evil presence coming toward them in the darkness.

Traveling down the road toward London was a group of Austrian born gypsies who are close by our group's camp. One of the horses pulling their wagon stumbles in the darkness, or so it seems. This wakes our merry band from the beginnings of their night's rest. Together they walk out to the road to see what has caused the commotion that has roused them from their slumber. There they encounter the band of gypsies looking to the needs of their presumably lame horse.

When the king of the gypsies sees Penelope and the young men standing at the edge of the road, he introduces himself and the others with him and tells them that their lead horse had taken a stone in his shoe and needs to rest for a time before they can continue their journey to London. Penelope, Prince Gregory and the triplets quickly invite this group to share their fire for the remainder of the night to allow the gypsies' horse the rest needed to recover from this pain.

Prince Gregory quickly takes the leadership role for Penelope and her entourage. "The fire is warm. Please ladies, join the fair Penelope close by there and stay warm in your night's rest," he invited, "And you men are welcome to join the four of us yonder at the edge of the forest, thus giving our women a bit of privacy they so richly deserve."

"Thank you, kind sir," Replied the King of the gypsies; "we would be honoured to join you for the remainder of the night to rest ourselves and our horses.

Little did our group know of the danger they were really in. For this band of gypsies were involved in the sale of young women as wives for the harem of the Maharajah of a small province in

Eastern India. They had sent a scout out ahead of their wagon to locate young, unsuspecting women to abduct and sell to the Maharajah. This scout had been lurking in the forest as Penelope and the young men had bedded down for the night. When all was quiet at the campsite, he ran back to the gypsies' wagon to tell their king of the beautiful young woman traveling in the company of four young men that were even now asleep just off the road about 20 minutes away.

So the king of the gypsies made the plan for the horse to "go lame" right at that point of the road so that they could "camp" there by Penelope and the young men and then be in a position to steal her away while Prince Gregory and the triplets slept through the night.

As soon as our young men were fast asleep again the king made the signal to the women of his band. They quickly and quietly wrapped Penelope up in some blankets, tied her with their bandanas and carried her to their wagon. Meanwhile the gypsy men were quietly hitching the horse and wagon. When all was in preparation they moved out on to the road and resumed their journey to meet the ship at the Thames River in London.

About an hour into their journey the gypsy king decided that they would change directions and take an alternate road into London as it would shorten the journey by about half a day. He also had one of the young men following behind the wagon to assure its tracks were not visible to anyone who might choose to follow them.

~*~

When the young men woke at dawn they discovered the treachery that had been brought upon Penelope. Prince Gregory, having fallen in love with Penelope and having assumed the role of our group's leader when the gypsies came upon their camp, felt very guilty at not having protected her from being kidnapped. He now was seeking the help of the triplets in tracking the gypsy's wagon as they were well versed in hunting and tracking animals in order to feed their family and the manor house in the hamlet of Leedsfield.

Penelope's Perils

"How could I have been so stupid," Gregory fumed when they discovered Penelope missing, "We all should have slept close by the fire to protect the fair Penelope. Then we would have heard them when they were abducting her."

"Now there, Gregory," comforted James, "How could we have known these people meant us harm. They appeared to be travelers in need of assistance with their lame horse. You could not have known what they were up to."

"That's right," George quipped, "but we should mount up and head out to search for her. Godfrey is the best tracker and hunter. He should be the point."

All were agreed and they immediately mounted their horses and galloped off in search of the gypsy band and our Penelope. Godfrey took the point and rode a little ahead of the rest of our young men. He noticed that the tracks weren't consistent on the road they were following. They seemed to run for a few hundred yards and then disappear for a while, only to reappear a mile or so down the road. But with his keen eye he was able to follow them into the next village were they were obliterated by the traffic of the locals since by now the sun was high in the sky and the village was a buzz with its daily activity. The loss of tracks to follow greatly disturbed our band of heroes. With no clear guidance and two possible roads to choose, they decided to split up. So they stopped for a brief break to share the remaining biscuits and fruit from their stay with the woman and her daughter.

After eating and refreshing themselves with a cool drink from the village well James and George took the road to the east while Godfrey and Gregory headed south toward London. They had decided that each pair would ride for half a day and if there were no sign of the gypsy wagon they would turn around and head back to the village to join the other team.

James and George traveled for about five hours with no luck in tracking the wagon they were in pursuit of. So they stopped to give the horses a rest and eat some of the local wild berries before they decided to turn around and head back for the village and the rest of their group.

Meanwhile Godfrey and Gregory had ridden hard and fast in search of the kidnappers and after about four hours the came upon their tracks once again. The scout for the gypsies felt they had a large enough head start and after the confusion of the village they had passed through earlier that morning, he had gotten lazy in trying to hide their tracks, therefore making Godfrey's job easier.

About 30 minutes after picking up the trail once again Godfrey and Gregory stopped to give the horses a much-needed rest and a drink at the stream just off the road. There they decided to refresh themselves as well. So they sat beneath a large tree at the edge of the stream and shared another of the biscuits remaining from their meal the night before.

As the pair was taking their rest, James and George had sought the assistance of a local farmer for a possible short cut back to the London road. The farmer told these brothers to ride through his pastureland into the forest always heading in a southwest direction and they would come to the road they sought in about three hours time. They got a drink from the farmer's well, thanked him again and were off following the directions he had given. By riding hard all day and long into the night, and taking infrequent and short rests, this pair met up with the other pair a couple of hours before the breaking of the new day. So they dismounted and reigned in their horses and joined the other two at the campfire for a short, but much needed rest.

About two hours after dawn, our foursome being rested they once again set off in the direction of London in search of the gypsies and Penelope. All day and long into their second night on the road back to London they came to a small roadside inn, the same one where Penelope had heard the plans of Gregory's brother to assonate the King. The horses needing rest and they themselves wanting a respite, they decide to stop for a few hours. Not wanting to draw attention to themselves, they went behind the inn to put the horses in the coral and to bed down for the night on the hay in the barn.

Drawing up to the barn they see a light in the distance, so our band of "brothers" leave the horses and quietly sneak through the trees to check this out. Crouching in the trees behind the stable and barn they see that the light is a large campfire and behind the fire is the gypsy's wagon. No one is in sight, so they quietly sneak back to the barn to make their plans for rescuing Penelope.

Penelope's Perils

Chapter Eight
Planning Penelope's Rescue

While the gypsies were traveling toward London and the ship awaiting them at the dock on the Thames River they were not sedentary. The women of the family had taken Penelope under wings to teach her some lessons in what they called the "womanly arts," that being how to dress, talk and act like a lady. And how to apply kohl to her eyes and rouge to her fair cheeks to accentuate her natural beauty. The grandmother of the band felt especially drawn Penelope and started to share her many years of experience with our heroine to prepare her for what she considered a high honor and calling for any woman, that of being the wife of a Maharaja; a queen among his people.

"Darling, "she began, "you must wash your face till is gleams in its rosy beauty. And brush your fair hair until it shines forth as the gold in the treasuries of the king. It is just as important for a woman to maintain her outward beauty as it is to preserve your purity for the most important night of your life, that being the night you are wed."

Grandmother spoke many sage words to Penelope as they traveled. And she took each one for what truths it contained and hid these truths in her heart.

In the hours they rode together the women pooled their worldly wealth to bedeck their captive in a manner they thought was befitting her future position as a middle-eastern Maharani. Penelope was dressed in a white lace peasant blouse over many lace and silk petticoats, covered by a ruby red skirt embroidered with brilliantly plumed peacocks around its hemline, which just dragged the ground. Celeste, the oldest, placed an emerald tiara on her head and earrings to match; which brought out the fiery green of her eyes behind their new rims of kohl. Rosa, their shy, lanky and sometimes awkward, middle sister layered Penelope with many strands of gold, as well as a string of pearls for her throat and its mate to wrap around Penelope's ankle. Sylvia, the youngest sister, brought out her most prized possession and tied it around Penelope's slim waist; it was a long silk scarf of multiple shades of green that blended well with the peacock trim of her newly donned skirt and the fiery green of her eyes. To complete the picture, Grandmother gave her an ivory cross to wear around her neck and her very own prayer book, which she advised Penelope to hide in the pocket of her blouse.

"These, my young friend," Grandmother whispered, "will protect you as your journey into womanhood continues. Pray to the Lord of the cross often and meditate upon the prayers of this book for comfort in times of trouble and for solace in a world were peace is often rare."

Now dressed in all her finery, Penelope listened as the women talked of the life they each thought she was soon to be entering into. They described the dark and rugged looks of the Maharaja, whom they said was tall, dark and very handsome. But Penelope's thoughts kept drifting back to the band of "brothers" she had been taken from, but especially to the face of Gregory. Its kind soft lines, raven colored hair, and eyes of deep violet, like the tranquil pools found throughout the forest surrounding he father's estate. She found in its memory a place of peace as she recalled the times they had shared in saving the life of the king and their many other recent adventures and victories.

She wondered if the young men she had been taken away from were following the trail of her captives' wagon, if they were close by and when they would rescue her from this rolling prison. Oh, it wasn't a cruel captivity; in reality the women were very kind and loving toward her. But she was being taken against her will to become one of the wives of a man she didn't know, and in fact had never met. And if they didn't arrive soon, she feared she would never see her home and father again, let alone these brave young men she had come to love as her very family. So she prayed as the Grandmother had advised, to the Lord of all - Jesus, to bring a quick and happy end to this time of trial and captivity.

~*~

Penelope's Perils

If you remember we left our valiant young men near the barn behind the roadside inn where Penelope had first learned the details of the deadly assault on the king planned by Gregory's brother, Steven.

The Gypsies were sleeping soundly, having forgotten all about the four young men they had left behind when they abducted the Lady Penelope. The women and Penelope were sleeping inside the wagon, while the King of the Gypsies and his chief assistant, and oldest son, were sleeping close by the fire. The young scout was sitting by a near-by tree, sleeping while he was supposed to be keeping watch over the camp for intruders of any kind.

Sizing up the situation, Gregory led the triplets back into the cover of the forest to devise a plan that would bring about the rescue of Penelope and get the gypsy tribe locked up by the county bailiff until the itinerant judge came into the district to hold his regular session of hearings.

"I want the three of you to hide in the trees around the wagon," Gregory started, "When I make a soft cough I want you to start making loud noises like a wild bears. Rattle the trees and sound like you are going to tear them down and destroy the wagon. When the men start into the forest, lead them away from the wagon.

While you keep the other men busy, I am going to grab the King and take him away. After about 10 minutes, before the men catch up to you, get real quiet and hide in the brush. When you hear them give up their search for you, return and meet me behind the stable of the Inn. When they will discover the King missing they will begin to search for him. As it is dark, they will give up quickly and decide to wait until daylight to begin their search again. When they gather at dawn, I will be nearby and call their attention to myself and tell them I have their King and offer to trade him for Penelope."

The triplets were in agreement with Gregory's plan so they went about to do as he had proposed, one to the East side of the wagon one to the South the other to the West side. Gregory waited at the

North side of the camp until the others where well in to their destructive attack. James, Godfrey & George started making their bear noises in their various places and the men of the gypsy band woke up startled. After gaining their bearings, the gypsy men decided to split up to locate the cause of all the commotion and to put an end of it to save their wagon and its contents. They followed the noises deep into the forest, wandering after the "wild bear" brothers.

Meanwhile, inside the wagon the women stir and strain to hear what is happening.

Grandmother whispers, "Ladies, no noise. We don't want to invite that wild animal in here."

So the women remained as still as church mice until all was calm and quiet. Eventually they all drifted off to sleep again.

The triplets are successful in leading away the men folk of the gypsy group. So successful that they themselves get lost in the woods and have to lay still in the underbrush to hide until the first light so they can find their way back to the stable. But Gregory has managed to blindfold and tie up the gypsy King and lead him away into the stable. He cleared a large area of the floor near one of the upright beams, tied the King to the beam and covered him in fresh straw to keep him warm and to hide him from anyone who may happen into the stable. Next he hides in the shadows to await the return of the three brothers.

Penelope's Perils

Chapter Nine
Penelope's Rescue?

The men of the gypsy band returned to their camp only to find that their King has disappeared. They searched briefly around the camp area, but as it was a starless night and very dark they decided to return to the campfire for a couple hours rest before beginning to search again in earnest.

With the dawn our brothers three quietly crawled into the shadowed recesses of the stable to await the morning. Here they stay to make sure no one comes in to look for the gypsy king.

When the sun was high in the country sky the men of the gypsy camp arose to start their day. As the women came from the wagon to begin preparing their breakfast, Gregory stands on a rock about 30 feet away from the fire, above the camp. He continues to watch the group eat their meal and clean up. The women have started back into the wagon as the men folk prepare to leave the camp to search for their king, Gregory yells to get their attention.

"Who is in charge here?" Gregory shouts.

The oldest of the gypsy clan steps forward. "Our father is missing, I am leading in his absence," he replies.

"I know where your father is. I will have him returned to you when you return to me the Lady Penelope."

"We will make no trade with you! The girl is ours. We have made a deal to send her abroad"

As they discuss the gypsy king's return Penelope turns at the door of the wagon to look into the eyes of Gregory standing on the rock. The Grandmother sees the look of love in her eyes as Penelope watches the men's exchange of words. She senses what Penelope has not spoken to anyone, only to her dreams, she is in love with Prince Gregory. Grandmother quickly and quietly rushed the women into the wagon. She huddles close to her granddaughters to tell them her plan.

"My darlings," Grandmother began, "this lady is in love with the gallant lad holding our king and father. We must re-unite the young lovers and free our king. These men will never come to a quick and peaceful solution."

So the gypsy women snuck Penelope out the rear door of the wagon huddled in their midst and covered with a hooded cloak. They led her through the forest to the stable where the triplets were holding the king. Inside they released Penelope and spoke to James and convinced him and his brothers to release the king. Together the triplets, the gypsy women, Penelope and the king walked back to the camp and the arguing men.

"What is the meaning of all this fighting?" The king yelled as he entered the camp.

Immediately Gregory and the gypsy men stopped arguing and turned toward his voice. Penelope ran toward Gregory and threw her arms around his neck.

"My hero," she cried.

Gregory, in shock from seeing her with the brothers, the king and the gypsy women, stared at her and mumbled some unintelligible words.

The grandmother had explained to the king that the couple was in love and that they should release Penelope to him and the brothers and let them continue their journey. The king seeing the sense of this gathered all of the gypsies together with the triplets, Gregory and Penelope and made this announcement:

"It seems more is at stake here that the loss of our would be Maharini. I have it on good authority that the Lady Penelope and the good Prince Gregory have found true love and should be allowed to explore the possibility of a marital relationship. Far be

it from me to hinder the progress of true love. I hereby release
Penelope and beg forgiveness of her and her traveling companions
for taking her and thus delaying their travels."

After the king's speech there was lots hugging and backslapping.
The gypsy women made a quick meal for the whole group and all
sat down to eat in peace. After the meal, our merry entourage
made their way back to the highway and headed toward the hamlet
of Leedsfield. The brothers had decided not to turn the gypsies
over to the bailiff as the king gave his word they would never take
another girl away from their home and family. The king was a
believer in the man of the cross, so the band of friends thought they
could trust his word. The gypsy women asked Penelope to keep
their gifts in a form of restitution for them having abducted her.
With Penelope and her entourage back on the road home, the
gypsies had to make some decisions on how they were going to
make the money needed to keep them afloat without the
kidnapping scheme to provide their income. So they continued to
camp there behind the Inn for a few days to make their plans.

Our merry band is now riding double time to make up for the lost
days on the trail, and is quickly fading off into the distance, beyond
the sight of the gypsy troupe.

Penelope's Perils

Chapter Ten
The Road Home

Dawn brings our group closed to their goal of the hamlet of Leedsfield and home. Penelope and the boys woke to a breakfast of leftovers from the meal they had shared with the gypsy troupe the day before, after having spent the night in a meadow beside the road. Packing their leftovers in their saddlebags, they mounted their horses and fly like the wind north toward home and their respective parents. The day looked to be a beautiful one, the sun was beginning to peer over the treetops and our youthful travelers were riding hard and fast to make up for the long delay of Penelope's last peril.

As they rode the day grew warm and the horses began to tire due to their prolonged top speed. In order to preserve their ability to maintain their pace they took short breaks about every two to three hours to refresh the horses and quench their thirst from the dust and to unwind from the horseback. It was on one of these rests that our brothers four were tossing around one of their knapsacks like a ball at the edge of the pond in the meadow they had chosen to take their rest. Gregory missed George's toss and fell head long in the pond. Riotous laughter erupted from Penelope and the others as Gregory struggled to right himself.

"Look!" Gregory yelled, as he peered into the violet pool. "There's something gold and sparkling here."

At his words Gregory reached down into the pond and pulled at a golden chain. It was very hard going, as it was deep within the silt-covered bottom of the pond. Seeing the difficulty Gregory was having in retrieving the gold chain the brothers run to his side to offer their help.

"It's stuck, James," Gregory yelled. "Here, give me your knife so I can dig it out."

He dug around it with James' knife and after about 15 minutes of hard digging he finally released the chain from its watery holding tank. When Gregory lifted his treasure from the pond it was caked with loads of mud. As he used the edge of the knapsack to clean this find he saw that it was a 24 inch gold chain bearing a diamond and ruby encrusted, heart-shaped pendant. As they were miles from and hamlet or village and there were no houses nearby, and given its deep former location in the pond, our band thought to inquire on whom its owner may be with the bailiff of the next village. Quickly mounting their horses again, our merry brigade headed north towards home once more.

Traveling once again at their breakneck pace, our group entered the sought out hamlet, some ten miles from their pond side respite in about two hours time. Wanting to find the rightful owner of his trophy, Gregory heads toward the bailiff's office after tying their mounts to the rail of the inn. Meanwhile the triplets and Lady Penelope entered the market to buy supplies for the last two days of their journey and get some of the news from the locals. Penelope purchased bread, fruit and dried meat from the local vendors as Godfrey escorted her, while James and George looked in at the pub for local news.

Gregory entered the bailiff's office and found him napping on the cot in his holding cell. Rousting him unceremoniously, Gregory poured them each a cup of coffee from the pot on the stove. Setting the mugs on the desk Gregory started his tail of finding the bejeweled necklace in the pond back down the road.

"Sir," Gregory started, "as we were resting near the pond back about ten miles, I noticed this shinny thing in the water. After considerable digging I unearthed a very beautiful necklace."

Pulling the treasure out of his knapsack Gregory handed it to the Bailiff.

"Well young man," The Bailiff began, "Local legend says a Lady and a Highwayman were traveling through the countryside 25 years ago. The Highwayman had abducted the lady from her home in the woods about five miles up the highway. As the bandit left the manor house with the lady she struggled all the way, kicking over a lamp in the hall. The manor house burned down killing the Lord of the manor and his servants, and the surrounding out buildings. The Lady put up a valiant fight as they rode away from the house but the highwayman did manage to subdue her down by the pond. The man didn't want to hurt the Lady; he had been secretly in love with her since his youth. He had known that a relationship was out of the question from the beginning as he was the son of a local farmer and she the daughter of a wealthy Lord. So he watched her from afar and when he saw an opportune time he stole into her father's house and carried her off. This necklace was around her neck on that fateful night and was reported missing when the Lady was rescued some time later."

"Is this lady still living?" Gregory asked

"The local men built her a cottage on her father's land to the West fork off the highway when she was rescued." The Bailiff replied. "She lives there with a man servant and a hired girl. Please visit her to return her necklace."

As Gregory was leaving the Bailiff's office his mind was foggy from the tale the Bailiff had recounted, to the point that he nearly ran into Penelope and her armload of supplies. Blushing, he mumbles his apology and sidesteps to avoid the collision. He quickly tells the rest of the group the story of the necklace as they walk back to the inn where their horses are tied. They ride together north and follow the West fork of the highway to the cottage of the lady who had lost this treasure so many years ago.

Pulling into the wide drive our merry band feels the shadows of a haunting past that surround this meager dwelling. As they dismount they are met in yard by a large hunting dog and the male servant the Bailiff had told Gregory about. When they inquired after seeing the lady of the house, he tried to dissuade them on visiting the lady. Gregory was insistent on seeing the lady, however the rest of our happy entourage was content to wait in the yard for his return. This seemed to clam the servant and he consented to let Gregory in to visit with the lady.

Having been shown into her parlor, Gregory paced the small room as he awaited the lady of the golden necklace. The moment she entered Gregory felt that he was in the presence of nobility, although her meager surroundings did little to give this impression; but the way she carried herself bore out her noble heritage. This did little to help Gregory's nervousness at the task he must perform, that of returning her lost necklace.

"Madame," He began, "I have found something of great value that I was told belongs to you."

As he stammers through this announcement, he reaches into his knapsack to retrieve the long lost necklace. Handing it to the lady she nearly faints at the sight of it. Gregory drops the necklace and catches the lady before she hits the floor. Laying her on the couch, he calls for her hired girl.

"No," she whispers, "I was just a little startled at the sight of that bauble lost so long ago and under such tragic conditions. That necklace once belonged to my mother, the former lady of this manor. She died in childbirth many years ago and I never knew her. But the reason for my weakened collapse is the circumstances of its loss."

"Yes, Madame," Gregory started, "I know of the conditions surrounding its loss. I spent the afternoon in town with the Bailiff and he advised me of the history surrounding the loss of your mother's necklace. I realized it must be of great worth so I wanted to return it to its rightful owner, that being you."

About this time the hired girl entered closely followed by the manservant, Penelope and the triplets, for they heard the lady scream just before her swoon. The lady, upon seeing Penelope eying her and Gregory in their close proximity, sensed there might be a relationship between the couple.

"I am truly sorry for my outburst," She announced to those who had just entered. "I have had a small fright. But I am OK, there is no need to remain."

The manservant led the others out the parlor door, but the lady requested Gregory to remain behind so they could finish their conversation.

"Young man," the lady began, "I have no desire to keep this necklace. It holds such deep and tragic memories that I could not bear to have it in my presence. For your honesty and valour I ask that you keep it as my gift. I fear you made have more need of it than I." And with that the lady dismissed Prince Gregory, as she was quite fatigued from the ordeal.

Gregory did not share the outcome of his time with this fine lady. He placed the necklace in the velvet pouch the lady had given him, for this is where she had kept it before its tragic loss. This pouch he hung around his neck and placed under his tunic, close to his heart. It was then that he decided to present it to the Lady Penelope as a token and pledge of his love and a promise to marry her. But he kept his intentions in his heart until the time was right.

Once again on the trail to Leedsfield our happy band continued their journey home.

At this time Sir Rolfe was beginning to worry about where his daughter and her brave escorts had gone. He had left them just outside London better than a fortnight ago with the pretense of heading home and to the surrounding outposts of the King to see how all was faring. But he had been home for now for the best part of a week and has yet to hear anything of their journey, let alone to see Penelope's arrival safe at the manor house. I say his pretense was to check on the Kings affairs, yet while he traveled to these out posts he had a second, more personal goal for his travels. He was also seeking a knight of great valour to be his son-in-law, for Penelope was quickly coming into her womanhood and of an age to marry.

Penelope's Perils

While on his journey Sir Rolf had met three such knights in the nearby outposts and has set a date for a great feast and "coming out" celebration for his lovely daughter.

"What has kept them from coming?" He asked aloud to no one in particular. "Have they befallen some danger along the way?"

Rolfe was quickly coming to the conclusion that he should get together the men of the hamlet to search for our merry entourage.

"They should have been here days ago." He sulked.

Just as he spoke those words a post rider sped in the gate and jumped from his horse. He spied Sir Rolfe standing in the courtyard and ran to meet him, and handed him an envelope. Rolfe hurriedly opened the letter and scanned its contents.

"Gallant Sir," it read, "due to unforeseen circumstances we have been delayed in our travels. We expect to arrive at mid-day on Tuesday next..."

"Why that's tomorrow!" Rolfe exclaimed

Rolfe raced around the estate to make sure all was in readiness for the arrival of Lady Penelope and her entourage. He spoke to the cook and asked her to prepare all of Penelope's favorite foods. Next he had the housekeeper open her bedroom windows to freshen it for Penelope's return. The gardener was consulted on fresh arrangements to place about the manor house to brighten it for the Lady of the house's return.

Rolfe thought to go hunting to bring in a buck to roast for Penelope's arrival. As time was quickly escaping for him, Rolfe sent his gamekeeper out to get the venison for their celebration so that he could oversee the final preparations. When the sun was slowly drifting behind the western horizon all was finally in readiness for the festivities on the morrow. The venison was slowly roasting on a spit behind the manor house kitchen as a page turned the crank handle through the night to be relieved at dawn by

Rolfe's junior squire. The manor house was bedecked with flowers in every possible nook filling the whole manor with their beautiful fragrance. Penelope's bed was changed and the windows open to allow the breezes to continue to fill the air with their freshness. Rolfe judged all to be perfect for the celebration of her long awaited return, including the Knights he had previously interviewed as possible suitors for Penelope's hand. When he had made one final walk through of the yards and manor house, Rolfe adjourned to his bed for a bit of respite before the dawn and all the excitement it would bring.

With the rising of the sun our merry brigade rose and ate the last of their supplies, washed up in the nearby stream and mounted their steeds for the last leg of their journey. Eagerly anticipating their arrival in Leedsfield, Penelope and the triplets chattered away about what they have missed during their absence. However Gregory was not as enthusiastic about their arrival. He was in fact a bit green at the thought of their journey coming to an end. His fear was not in ending the journey as much as facing Sir Rolfe to ask his permission to court and marry the Lady Penelope. He stayed introspective as they rode and each mile of their journey made them closer to what he perceived as his impending doom. As noon approached our heroes stopped in a glen to give their horses a brief rest to refresh them for the final approach to the hamlet of Leedsfield. The triplets led their horses to the stream at the far side of the glen so Penelope took a moment to speak to Gregory.

"Why are you so quiet and distant," Penelope asked

"My Lady," Gregory began, "I am fearful at the prospect of meeting your father once again."

"Why, Gregory?" Penelope questioned, "You met him before in London and when we had foiled your brother's attempt to kill the King. Why would you be afraid to visit him in our home."

"My fair Lady," Gregory continued, "It isn't that I am afraid of seeing him again. It is a matter of greatest importance that I wish to discuss with him."

"What subject could you have to discuss with my father that would distress you, Sir?"

"My Lady, I would rather not share this with you until I have spoken to your father. It is a matter of conscience that I not speak on this subject until I have the privilege of a conversation on this matter with him."

"My dear Gregory, you should fret over any matter you feel the need to discuss with my father. He is a wise, loving and caring man and would do nothing to harm you. Besides, he likes you. I could tell by the way he patted you on the back and almost knocked you over. So, don't worry about meeting with him, it will be OK!"

By this time the horses were well watered and rested, so they all remounted and took up their double fast pace in order to reach the manor before the sunset on this lovely day.

The day was quickly drawing to an end and Sir Rolfe had dinner about ready to serve. The knights had all arrived and were on the lawn behind the manor house awaiting Rolfe's signal that Penelope had arrived and all was in readiness. Sir Rolfe was pacing the front drive in great expectation of our merry band's arrival.

Upon the horizon Rolfe sees a cloud of dust and a group of mounted figures approaching quickly. Straining his eyes, Rolfe to tries to find his daughter among the party, to no avail. He continues his pacing in anticipation.

As the sun hides behind the distant mountains our pacing father's mind is set to rest; for Penelope and her valiant escorts enter the gate and ride up the long drive to the manor house. She immediately jumps from her mount and runs to embrace Sir Rolfe in an enormous bear hug, both laughing and crying together at her being home once more.

Penelope's Perils

Chapter Eleven
Gregory Speaks to Sir Rolfe

After dinner when they had retired to the parlor for coffee, Gregory took his opportunity to approach Sir Rolfe. Shaking almost visibly, he requested a private word with Penelope's father, so the two of them adjourn to his library for their talk. Meanwhile the visiting knights are all vying for the attentions of our young Lady of the manor. Each of these knights is trying to out do the other in relating to her tales of their manly exploits on their various missions for the King. The triplets are sitting quietly by, smiling at their endeavors to impress our heroine. Each had marvelous tales of the missions they had been on to keep England safe from various threats of danger, but Penelope was not impressed. She simply chatted with her would be suitors in an effort to keep from immense boredom. She did not regale them with the many adventures she had enjoyed while she had traveled the countryside with her four gallant escorts. All the things they were trying to impress Penelope with didn't seem as fantastic as anything she and her entourage had encountered, so she just politely smiled and nodded in reply.

In the library Gregory was trying to get up the nerve to ask for Penelope's hand in marriage.

"Sir," Gregory began, "As you know I have spent considerable time with the Lady Penelope since meeting her in London a few weeks ago."

"Yes, Gregory," Rolfe replied, "I know you were instrumental in helping to save the life of our King and for protecting Penelope on the trip home from London."

"Sir I have become quite fond of you daughter." Gregory continued, "She is very lovely."

"Yes, Penelope has grown into a beautiful young woman," Rolfe agreed.

"Sir I have fallen in love with your daughter and would like your permission to marry her!" Gregory blurted out.

"Well, young man," Rolfe began, "I see you as a suitable suitor for her hand. Yet I don't know her thoughts on the matter at this time. I also feel she is too young to make a decision of this magnitude on her own. I will require speaking to her in private and finding her mind on this proposal. Then if she is agreeable I will set the terms for your betrothal period.

Gregory was agreeable with all that Rolfe asked on his impending betrothal to Lady Penelope. He was totally amazed that he had actually been able to make his intentions made to her father without collapsing in the process. When their conversation was at an end they rejoined the group in the parlor and Rolfe had a fresh pot of coffee brought in. As Rolfe had decided not to approach Penelope with the proposal that Gregory had made for her hand until the morrow, he asked Gregory to also refrain from discussing it with her as well. And Gregory agreed.

As the hour was getting late, Rolfe asked all of his guests to lodge within the manor house for the evening and share breakfast with himself and Penelope before taking their leave on the morrow. He hadn't shared his reasons for the invitations he gave to the young knights he had invited to share dinner that evening, so they had no idea he had meant to parade them as potential candidates for Penelope's heart and hand. They had thought his only idea was to spend time with others in service to the King, as he was. And they were happy to oblige him in accepting this invitation. They were likewise happy to stay the night and share breakfast with him and Penelope and their other guests as the outposts they were stationed at didn't dine on as elegant a fare as Sir Rolfe had served.

After another hour of light conversation and coffee, Lady Penelope excused herself and retired to her room. At this departure they all left the parlor and made to their various rooms within the manor house.

Penelope's Perils

At breakfast the next morning Sir Rolfe met with all of his guests and begged Penelope's forgiveness at her absence. The length of the journey home and all of their adventures had left her quite fatigued so she slept late and requested a tray in her room at mid-morning. Having dismissed his knights and seen the triplets depart; Rolfe and Gregory were once more alone. Together they went about the estate and completed the various chores that needed Rolfe's attention. They had just finished turning loose the flocks and were cleaning up for their midday meal when Penelope came out the front door of the manor. Having removed his tunic to wash up, Gregory quickly dashed inside the barn to cover himself before speaking to the young Lady.

"Good afternoon, my Lady," Gregory began, "I hope you rested well."

"Oh, Gregory, don't act so formal." Penelope laughed, "I am well rested. What have you and father been up to this beautiful day?"

"We have seen to the horses and moved the sheep out of the pen into the South pasture. Are you ready to join us for dinner?"

"Yes, cook has set a lovely table full of cold meats, cheeses and fresh vegetables. I was just coming to tell you and father all was in readiness. Come inside!"

Penelope led Gregory into the dining room and seated him across from her at the table. Sir Rolfe joined them a few minutes later and they enjoyed their cold meal while sharing the latest news of the hamlet of Leedsfield.

After their meal Gregory went for a ride over the lands of the estate while Sir Rolfe and Penelope spent some time together in the library. Gregory wanted to give the father and daughter some space so that Sir Rolfe could inquire on her feelings toward his proposal. He didn't want to appear too anxious for an answer, or maybe he was afraid of what her answer would be. At any rate he took off and rode across her father's lands until just before dark. Having been an avid huntsman before leaving home for the

London tournaments months ago Gregory enjoyed having the time to jump the streams and hedgerows while exploring the country surrounding the estate He let the horse take its head and he came to a nice meadow about an hour away from the house. Just as the sun was beginning to disappear behind the horizon Gregory headed back to the manor to wash-up and change clothes for the evening meal.

Once the three of them were seated at the table for supper Sir Rolfe had dinner served. They had a delicious meal of roast pheasant and wild rice with garden vegetables. There was little conversation during their meal as all present were caught up in their own thoughts. Dessert was held until coffee was served in the parlor and the three of them had relaxed for a time. Cook served fresh fruit and cheese slices along with the evening coffee and was promptly dismissed by Sir Rolfe for the night. When the three of them were alone in the parlor and all the servants had been dismissed for the night Sir Rolfe stood to address the young people.

"Gregory," He began, "I have spoken to Penelope about your proposal. And while it seems that she is quite taken with you, too, I am afraid I will have to delay your betrothal for the space of six months. I fear that the two of you are too young to be considering a commitment of this nature for the present. So I would like to request that you hold your peace and not commit to your betrothal at this time. During this six month delay I would like for you to promise to be faithful to the Lady in preparation for your marriage and return to your country to make a place for my daughter in your kingdom, home and heart. Further I am requesting Penelope to spend a time with a family close by here to be trained by the Lady of the manor in all the necessary arts of running a proper home. I have also asked her to remain faithful to you during your absence in preparation for your forth-coming betrothal, as well. If at the end of this six month delay your affections remain true toward each other I will permit a betrothal and eventual marriage between you and the young Lady."

"Sir," Gregory replied, "While I would like to wed Lady Penelope tomorrow, I will be bound by your recommendations. I will leave on the morrow for home and hearth to make the proper preparations for my Lady to join me upon our marriage."

Lady Penelope sat quietly as her father and Gregory discussed her future. When all was decided Penelope said good night to Gregory, kissed her father and disappeared up the stairs to her room.

Gregory and Sir Rolfe sat in the library and talked well into the night getting to know each other better in the short time they had left.

Penelope rose early the next morning to take a walk through the gardens before breakfast. As she walked Penelope picked a bouquet for roses to grace the breakfast table. As she wandered through the rose bushes she almost tripped over Gregory. She hadn't been paying attention to where she had wandered and he was crouched down between the bushes petting the kittens that wandered out from under the house looking for their morning bowl of milk. Gregory caught Penelope before she fell and helped her to right herself, standing to help her maintain her balance. She was terribly embarrassed by this near collision and it showed in her face with a bright red glow.

After brushing imaginary dirt from her dress, Penelope ran back into the kitchen with her bouquet of roses for cook to place in a vase on the table.

Thirty minutes later when Penelope and Gregory joined Sir Rolfe at the table for breakfast all evidence of their near collision was gone from both of their faces. The three of them had a quiet meal with very little small talk, as the couple was deep in thought over what the next six months would bring.

"Well, Gregory," Rolfe started to end the silence, "when do you plan to leave us?"

"Kind Sir, I will be leaving directly after breakfast. I feel the quicker I can return to my native land and make preparations, the faster this six month waiting period will end. I only have to saddle my horse and tie down my pack after breakfast."

"Very good, son," Rolfe replied, "I have ordered cook to load a pack with food for your journey. I know that the trip to London and the trip by boat will take more than a fortnight to complete. Please send a messenger to let us know that you have safely arrived in your homeport. And know that our hearts are with you in your absence."

After having said this Sir Rolfe excused himself from the table to return to his days work on the south end of the estate fixing fences.

When breakfast was at an end Penelope went to her room to mope while Gregory prepared for his departure. The thought of his leaving had made a void in her heart already, so she decided to spend her day alone.

Having fully loaded his steed, Gregory was ready to set out on his trip home, yet he longed to see the fair Penelope once more before he was to be so far removed from her for their six month waiting period. Penelope however was in no mood to be seen. Instead of coming down to see him off, Penelope stood in her bedroom window and waved her farewell from afar. She did, however send a letter down to him by her maid with directions for him not to open it until he was on the ship home. And thus she bid him adieu while waving out her bedroom window high above the estate drive as he rode off toward London and on to his faraway home in the Tyrol. Shortly after his departure, cook brought up an envelope atop the Velvet pouch Gregory had been given by the Lady of the Necklace and quickly returned to her kitchen post. Opening the envelope Penelope finds this note:

My dear Lady, within this pouch is a token of my pledge to return at the appointed time to ask for your hand in marriage. I would have enjoyed all the more to have delivered this pledge to you in person, however since you did not come to wish me well in my departure, I am left no choice but to deliver it at the hands of another. Farewell for now. Gregory.

Penelope's Perils

After having read his note Penelope opened the velvet pouch to discover the golden heart pendant covered with diamonds and rubies. She immediately placed the necklace around her neck and beneath the bodice of her dress so that it could remain close to her heart but hidden frmm the eyes of all.

~*~

After riding hard for four and half days Gregory arrived back in London. He went directly to the docks and booked passage on the next ship crossing the channel for France. As Tyrol is located in the mountainous region in the Alps near Switzerland taking the ship to France was the shortest route. His ship wasn't to disembark until the next morning at high tide, so Gregory went to a nearby inn to get a meal and a bit of rest until time for his ship to sail. Having asked the innkeeper to call him at sunrise Gregory mounted the stairs and closed himself in his room for the remainder of the day. He lay on the bed and tried to rest, but he continuously saw the sad figure of Lady Penelope in his mind whenever he closed his eyes. He hated having to leave her behind, but he knew this was a wise course of action in order to prepare for their life ahead.

~*~

Back at the manor house Penelope was still sad at the thought of six months with out seeing Gregory. However she took it in stride and set about to pack her bags for her stay with Lord and Lady Kensington. Sir Rolfe had ridden to their estate yesterday to inquire if Lady Penelope could come to learn from Lady Kensington the necessary lessons for running a proper household.

Sir Rolfe had also asked Lady Kensington to invite the eligible men of the surrounding area to any dinner party of other social event they might be holding. He was trying to give Penelope the advantage of her station by allowing the bachelors of their class to meet and get to know her in normal social settings. He wanted Penelope to have a choice of eligible suitors so that she could make a wise decision when it came time to pick a marriage partner. Rolfe thought Penelope and Gregory were too young to make a life commitment at this time. He also felt that they might find during their separation that they were not suited for one another after all.

Penelope's Perils

So in an effort to spare her from a life of spinsterhood, he wanted her to get to know other young men of her age and caliber.

Penelope had her portmanteau and valise loaded atop the carriage and climbed inside for the ride to Kensington Manor. She had requested to ride her own horse, but her father had insisted a Lady should travel in an enclosed carriage. He did consent to let her tie her horse to the carriage to accompany her to her destination. However he did not allow her to take her regular saddle. He had bought a sidesaddle for Penelope to replace the saddle she had grown up riding. He wanted Penelope to learn to behave like a Lady should.

After the bumpiest three-hour ride she had ever endured, Penelope arrived at Kensington Manor no worse for the wear. She is shown to her room and immediately sets about to unpack.

~*~

Having set sale a few hours ago, Gregory has returned to his cabin to dress for their midday meal. As he was pulling his fresh tunic from his pack he finds the letter that Penelope had given upon his departure. Losing track of the present, he sat on his bunk and opened the envelope. Pouring over the words she had written on the pages enclosed he fails to notice her lace handkerchief that drops to the floor as he reads:

"My Fine Prince; I fear that my father has forced this separation in an effort to prevent us from marrying. I have given you this handkerchief as a token of my pledge to remain true to you in purity of heart, mind and body. It saddens me to know we will be apart for such a long time, however I will write daily in an effort to make the days pass more quickly. Until you return, I am your faithful Penelope."

Having read and re-read Penelope's words 10 times, Gregory fell to the floor to recover the handkerchief sent by this fair Lady. Upon picking it up he placed it in the inner pocket of his tunic, close to his heart, there to remain until he would see her again.

Penelope's Perils

Having forgotten all about the meal he had started dressing for, Prince Gregory retired to his bunk to re-read once more, or perhaps 100 times, the note from Penelope.

Penelope's Perils

Chapter Twelve
Gregory's Return

The time for Penelope and Gregory's six-month separation now at an end. All was in readiness for the Prince to return to Sir Rolfe's estate and begin the promised betrothal of Lady Penelope. Penelope had learned well all that Lady Kensington had taught her on the proper management of a large estate. The Lady had returned a favorable report to Sir Rolfe when he arrived a few days ago to retrieve Penelope. Penelope was making her father's estate gleam in preparation for Gregory's return. She had already seen that the staff polished the banisters, the wall panels and the picture frames of all the family portraits hanging throughout the manor. She had also taken all the tapestries down had them placed outside over the hedgerows and had the dust beaten out of them. Everything looked fresh and clean throughout the manor. Now Penelope seemed to be at a loss for something to do. Gregory's ship had docked in London four days ago.

"Where is he? How come it is taking him so long to ride here? When we came together it only took us four and a half days. So, where is he?" Penelope was ranting through the estate grounds in impatience.

"Penelope," he father chided, "He will be here soon. Your pacing and ranting will not hurry him on his way. He sent a message from the London dock that he was going to be held up a day or two upon his return. My dear I know he will be here soon. Try not to worry!"

"Yes, Father, but I have missed him so much."

"I know daughter. But missing him will not make him arrive any faster than he can ride. I expect he will be here on the morrow. Come, let us go in to supper. Cook says it is getting cold and it will spoil if we don't eat it soon."

Resigned to the wisdom of her father, Penelope walked arm in arm with him into the manor and to the dining room table.

~*~

Meanwhile Prince Gregory was on his way to the hamlet of Leedsfield and the estate of Sir Rolfe. He had hired a carriage for this trip, instead of his typical horse. Gregory was trying to think ahead for when he and the fair Lady would leave the hamlet for their life together. On this forth night of his journey Gregory, being about one day's ride from the hamlet of Leedsfield, he had decided to spend this last night sleeping under the open sky, counting the stars to refresh his mind in peaceful sleep. He told the hired driver and footman that they could retire inside the coach for the evening after sharing a supper of brook trout and bread left over from his lunch with them.

Not being able to settle into sleep, Gregory decides to walk around the meadow he had chosen for their camp. Taking a torch from the fire's edge he heads toward the far side of the meadow. As he was wandering in the dark he was unable to see that the ground was very uneven and had many low spots. With his thoughts wandering back to the hamlet of Leedsfield and the estate of Sir Rolfe and his lovely daughter Lady Penelope, Gregory was not ready for the hole he had just fallen into. This fall brought our hero back from his mind's wandering and into the present as he landed with a great thud on his left leg.

"Help! Help! ...I've fallen and I can't get up!" Gregory screamed

Gregory yelled for what seemed like hours, yet was about 15 minutes, until his driver and footman had been wakened from their sleep. He had very great pain in his left leg from the fall and could not bear putting weight on it. The driver and footman each grabbed a torch from the fire and went off in the direction of Gregory's screams. Coming on him laying on the ground in the large, deep depression they immediately got down one on each side of him and together lifted him to a standing position balanced on his right foot. With Gregory between them they slowly walked him back to the carriage and placed him on the seat inside with the injured leg resting the seat opposite him. The driver then covered Gregory with the fur-lined lap robe. After making him as comfortable as possible, the driver and footman lit the lamps and once again set out for the hamlet of Leedsfield.

~*~

Penelope, having spent a sleepless night, rose with the sun. Splashing water on her face from the basin in her room, she dressed quickly and headed down the stairs. Anxious to start the day she went through the kitchen to the servant's quarters to rouse the cook and help her prepare their breakfast. Together she and cook laid out platters of cold meat, cheeses, and bread toasted over the coals of the cook fire. Next they prepared a pot of cornmeal mush and set this and the various platters on the sideboard in the dining hall. When all was in readiness she had cook sound the meal bell and went to take her place at the table to await her father's appearance at the table.

As Sir Rolfe was coming in from the stable he stopped at the well and drew a bucket of water to clean up before he went in to eat. As he was washing his face a carriage pulled in the driveway and came to a stop. The driver jumped from the box and opened the door to assist Prince Gregory in departing from the carriage. Rolfe, seeing the driver assisting Gregory immediately came up to his left side and together they propped up the young gentleman and helped him into the manor. Hearing the door open, Penelope got up from her chair and went to the door of the dining room. She was of a mind to reprimand her father for his tardiness in coming to breakfast; however, upon seeing the condition of Gregory, she immediately went into "nurse" mode. Penelope yelled for the servants to bring blankets and pillows into the Library. She had her father and the driver laid him on the sofa and sent the stable boy into the hamlet to fetch the doctor.

After having plumped Gregory's pillows and covered him with blankets, Penelope fixed a tray for him and herself and took them into the Library so they could eat together while they awaited the Doctor.

Rolfe ate his breakfast quickly and returned to the stable. Having his daughter fussing about like a mother hen reminded him of when he and his wife had first wed and he had caught a chill while out hunting for their winter meat. She had rushed him into his bed with a hot water bottle and kept checking on him what seemed like every other minute. He was so caught up in his remembering that he was nearly run over by the doctor's horse when he arrived. Shaken from his reverie he led the doctor into the Library grabbed Penelope by the hand and led her into the kitchen for a cup of coffee while the Doctor examined Gregory.

"What can be taking so long?" Penelope questioned, "He's been in there forever!"

"My girl," Sir Rolfe began, "Be patient. The doctor wants to be sure nothing is broken. You don't want him to miss anything, do you?"

"No, Father." Penelope replied. "I just want him to hurry. I guess I am just worried that something serious may be wrong. Oh Daddy, I'm so scared."

"I know, honey." Sir Rolfe answered, "We must trust the Maker of all that things will work out for the best for all concerned. Have Peace my child. The Maker and I will be with you through it all."

The Doctor spent about an hour with Gregory and when he came out of the Library he was smiling from ear to ear.

"It seems our patient has suffered more from a bruised ego than from the cuts and bruises on his arms and legs."

"Thank you, Doctor." Said Sir Rolfe, "How much do I owe you?"

"Sir," the Doctor replied, "the young Prince has taken care of the bill. There is nothing due. Young Lady, I have told Gregory that he is to stay abed for 3-5 days before he tries to do any walking on his battered legs."

"Yes, Doctor." Penelope replied, "What will he be able to do when he ready to get up and around."

"Dear Lady," The Doctor advised, "He should keep activity at a minimum for the first two weeks, just a gentle walk through the grounds for no longer than 15-20 minutes. If he is healing well, I will release him for full activities at that time.

"Thank you, Sir. I will make sure he is a model patient until you release him. He will not be happy with this information, but he will follow your directions."

"Thanks, Young Lady. I believe my patient is in good hands." Having said this, the Doctor left.

Penelope returned to the Library to finish her breakfast, remove the meal trays and plump Gregory's pillows again before going to the kitchen to check with cook on plans for their dinner meal.

While Penelope saw to the day's chores and Sir Rolfe was in the stable, Gregory had a stack of books set on the end table within reach. He had a variety of historical adventures and classical literature taken from the Library shelves in an effort to keep his mind active while his body was not able to be. He started reading a comical history of Germany that had him laughing so hard that he nearly fell off the sofa where he was laying. In fact, he knocked over the tray with his glass of water and some small cakes that was also setting on the end table beside the books. The crash of the tray was enough to bring Penelope running from the kitchen to check that all was OK with her patient.

"Are you alright?" Penelope asked, out of breath from her sprint.

"I am fine," Gregory replied. "I was just laughing so hard that I knocked over my snack tray and broke the saucer full of cakes.

Penelope cleaned up the mess, replaced the cakes with more, then asked Gregory if he would like to go out into the garden for some fresh air. Together, Gregory leaning on Penelope's arm, they walked through the rose garden, along the paths through the peony patch and around the gold fishpond back to the French doors leading into the Library. All of this took them only about 10 minutes, but Gregory was still a bit winded when he returned to his sofa to rest.

When Gregory was resettled on the sofa in the Library, Penelope went into the kitchen and asked cook if she would check in on him a couple of times during the next hour as she was going out for a ride on her favorite horse. Having been in such close quarters all day, she longed for the freedom of the open countryside and the wind in her long golden tresses. So refreshing was her ride that it allowed her to ponder all the things that were plaguing her of late. All the many lessons of running a large estate were starting to come into play in her care of Prince Gregory during his time of recovery from his late night fall on his journey here to Leedsfield and her fathers estate. She hadn't realized how important all of the little things that she had learned from Mrs. Kensington would be. So during this time of respite she allowed her mind to wander through these details to insure that all was being done to insure the proper care of not only her father's manor house and its grounds, but also of her patient.

~*~

Gregory's injuries healed quickly under the watchful eye and loving care of Lady Penelope. When the two weeks of bed rest prescribed by the Doctor were completed Gregory was anxious to be up and around. He inquired of Sir Rolfe as to what he could do about the estate to help pay for his keep since he had been there. Sir Rolfe asked that he lend a hand with the fencing that he was in process of repairing and Gregory gladly pitched in to get this job completed. Due to his recent injuries, Gregory wasn't able to do as much as he would like to. He was able to work at this project for about 2-3 hours daily at first, eventually building up to a full day within about 10 days time.

Penelope's Perils

Upon completion of the fencing repairs Sir Rolfe decided to throw a ball to honor Prince Gregory's visit. He also had in mind to present Lady Penelope to all the eligible young men of their area in an effort to give her opportunity to spend time with all the potential suitors around about them. Penelope and cook designed a wonderful menu of roast geese and all the trimmings for this gala event. She also had sent to London for a ball gown of emerald satin brocade trimmed with ivory lace and red rosettes.

On the day of this event Lady Penelope and Gregory sought to speak with Sir Rolfe before they went to dress for the evening. Meeting him in the Library they addressed him about the nature of this event.

"My kind Sir," Gregory started, "I feel that you do me a disservice. I thought that we had an agreement that upon completion of six months separation and preparation I would be given the privilege of marrying your lovely daughter.

"I do remember our agreement, fine sir; however I felt it necessary to give the Lady more suitable choices for a suitor before she made her decision on the man she would marry. I believe marriage is a commitment made for life and should be made after much consideration and prayer."

"Father," Penelope replied, "I, too, believe marriage to be a life long commitment. And I have made my choice of husbands. Even with all of the young men of the kingdom that have been at the various social functions I have attended, I have chosen Prince Gregory. My heart could never belong to another as it does to this gentleman that I have stood beside in battle as well as in his time of healing from his recent injuries. Please honor your pledge and allow us to announce our betrothal at the ball tonight."

"My dear Lady," her father replied, "I fear I am not worthy of my title at this moment. I see by your face as well as your words that your heart is true toward the fine Prince. I will permit the announcement this evening upon your entrance to the ball. However I will require at least a six-month betrothal before I will allow you and he to wed. I would like Gregory to remain here in our guest room for your betrothal period so that he is on hand to help you with all the arrangements for the wedding.

~*~

At the stroke of nine that evening the Grand Ballroom doors were opened to their full extent. Ladies and Gentlemen from all over England and most of Europe were present at this event, the only one of its kind in this manor house since Lady Madelaine's passing years ago. And now all were waiting in anticipation for the entrance of Lady Penelope. Standing at the great bay windows on the south end of the hall were Sir Rolfe and Prince Gregory. As the orchestra began playing the Tyrol national anthem a hush fell over the crowd. The dancers parted much like the Red Sea in the days of Moses, and Prince Gregory made his way through the room to escort the Lady Penelope into the hall.

The Prince was dressed in the costume of his native Tyrol, while Lady Penelope was wearing a beautiful emerald satin brocade trimmed with ivory lace and red rosettes. They danced their way through the throng back to the bay windows where Sir Rolfe was standing. As they reached him Sir Rolfe quieted the crowd and proceeded to speak.

"Good evening Ladies and Gentlemen." Rolfe began, "I wish to present to you the crown prince of Tyrol, Prince Gregory. I am very honored tonight to announce the engagement of the lovely Lady Penelope, my daughter, to this fine young man. They are to be wed just six months hence."

After Sir Rolfe's announcement there was much talking for the better part of 20 minutes, after which Lady Penelope went to the orchestra conductor and requested he play once more. Once the dancing resumed the group danced on until the wee hours of the morning. As the party finally broke up near the dawning of the new day, Sir Rolfe, having opened up all the guest rooms in preparation for this event, invited those living far from the hamlet to stay in one of these spare rooms.

Penelope's Perils

Epilogue
The Wedding

The nobility and royals invited to the wedding had arrived and were milling about the grand ballroom awaiting the entrance of Lady Penelope and Prince Gregory. Sir Rolfe was dressed in his best formal attire standing at the ready in front of the large bay windows on the south end of the room with the Vicar of the hamlet's church. The betrothal period had gone smoothly and the wedding was about to begin. Lady Penelope had made all of the arrangements in record time and actually had a couple days to spare before the grand event to rest in preparation for her most special moment.

The doors of the Grand Ballroom quietly swung open. Lady Penelope was dressed in an ivory lace dress last worn by her mother on her wedding day, hair beautifully coiffed and wearing the beautiful golden heart covered with diamonds and rubies, was on the arm of the Handsome Prince Gregory who was dressed in the military uniform of his native Tyrol. Slowly they descended the flower-bedecked staircase, crossed the entry hall and entered the Grand Ballroom as if on a great cloud. The room was hushed and in awe as the Vicar recited and the couple echoed their vows. Finally the silence erupted in a volley of applause as the Vicar proclaimed, "I now pronounce you man and wife. You may kiss your bride!"

~*~

Penelope and Gregory lived together very happily and enjoyed many more "Perils" and adventures together! Many of which lay Ahead for us in books to come...

Penelope's Perils

Penelope's Perils